Fear of the Beast

Joann Harris

Order this book online at www.trafford.com
or email orders@trafford.com

Most Trafford titles are also available at major online book retailers.

Printed in the United States of America.

ISBN: 978-1-4269-3440-7 (sc)
ISBN: 978-1-4269-3441-4 (ebk)

Our mission is to efficiently provide the world's finest, most comprehensive book publishing service, enabling every author to experience success. To find out how to publish your book, your way, and have it available worldwide, visit us online at www.trafford.com

Trafford rev. 08/28/2010

www.trafford.com

North America & international
toll-free: 1 888 232 4444 (USA & Canada)
phone: 250 383 6864 • fax: 812 355 4082

Prologue

The town of Wheatfield no longer exists. Very little of the northeastern part of Fork County exists, except in the memories of those who may once have lived there and were fortunate enough to be gone when the great fireball struck, searing the land for miles. Scientists were stunned by the suddenness of the huge fireball, for it seemed to materialize out of the heavens, traveling at such a tremendous speed, it was almost beyond calculation.

"Where had it come from?" the scientists were asked by a stunned population.

"From straight out of the sun," was the reply.

"You could not have predicted it?"

"No."

"Why?" The scientists hedged that question, for many of them were sworn avowed atheists. Finally, one man from an observatory in Washington who was not an unbeliever did reply, although not to the satisfaction of all his colleagues. His reply brought laughter from more than a few of his fellow scientists.

How does one predict when the hand of God will fall, and how hard the blow will be? If indeed it had been as the scientists said, the hand of God, it had been a mighty slap from him. By the time various spies in the skies satellites picked up on the cannonading mass of fiery destruction, it was all ready on top of the satellites, going through them, and burning them before they could be photographed, more than a one second shot at best, and transmit that to earth. Those pictures that did make it back to earth were immediately ordered to be seized by a presidential order.

Some said it was shaped like a Star of David. Others said it looked like an artist's conception of God's face; striking resemblance. The president told the scientists to shut their damned mouths, too, or face the prospects of never receiving another dime of government money for anything. But many people witnessed the strange blue lights that precede the crash of the, whatever the hell it was, and they asked about those lights. But suddenly all were quiet about the mighty ball of fire, except for speculation. That soon began to fade as the news pushed the holocaust out of the headlines. Only the insurance companies were left to ponder over the crash and dole out large sums of money to the relatives of those who had been killed. An astronomer in California thought he knew what had happened but he kept his mouth shut-not out of any fear of the government, but because he felt it was the right thing to do. One investigative fellow did put some rather interesting and curious events together after a bit of prowling. But since he was a career army reservist and did not wish to spend his summer obligations to Uncle Sam cleaning up gooney bird shit on Guam, he kept his mouth shut. Someday, maybe, he will write a book about it, and maybe by then he will believe it himself and be assured the protection of the Dalai Lama in some cave in Tibet.

What he had pieced together was that at almost the precise moment of fiery impact with earth, a series of fires leveled a huge man that was seen leaving earth, moving toward the heavens traveling at tremendous speed. No one knew what that thing was or if they did, they weren't saying, and there were some people who remained unaccounted for after the fire at the mansion. One of them was a young man by the name of Alex Balloon who was a minister in Wheatfield who had died under very mysterious circumstances back in '52 when another disaster had befallen that tragedy-ridden community, but the investigative reporter wisely closed his journal on both disasters for a time.

Late in the season. By this time in the eastern part of Nebraska there was usually a lash of winters approach in the air, a bit that brought color to the cheeks of pedestrians urgently but softly speaking of the harsh winter just ahead. But the winds that blew across the plains and rolling sand hills had a torrid touch and bra a sudden surliness to the people of this sparsely populated county, The few would learn too late. And out in the badlands some miles from Wheatfield, inside a fenced-in area where horror sprang to life back in the late 50's, something stirred. A creature cautiously stuck its head out of the hidden cave and looked around, viewing its surroundings through evil, red eyes. The beast had felt the hot fingers of the wind pushing through the cave entrance as a probing hand might do, signaling those which serve another master that it was time. The Dark One was near. The wind grew in strength and heat-the beast snarling in reply. The man like creature rose from its sentry position to crawl out of the filthy hole, rising to stand like human bits of dust and twigs and blowing sand striking its hairy body. But the beast to the beast it was a signal of love, a gesture of welcome. The beast roared its breath foul. It held its huge arms upward and shook its fists toward the sky, roaring its contempt for that God who occupies a more lofty position than the master of the beast. For the creature knew but one god: the Prince of Darkness, the Lord of the Flies, and Ruler of all that is Evil.

From behind the sentry came a guttural sound as other beasts rose from their long sleep, surly and hungry. They craved meat and the sweet taste of blood, but the sentry again tested the wind as the wind spoke its reply. The sentry held up one warning paw to those below, holding them at bay. He growled and the others drew back into the darkness of the evil smelling hole in the earth. They knew they must obey the master.. The growling sentry told them to wait-the master will tell us when we may move. Be patient for you have waited more than twenty years. Wai**t.**

It was in the summer of '54 when the horror finally surfaced, erupting like a too long festering boil spewing its corruption over all those near it, especially the town of Fork County. Those who survived the terror remembered it as the summer of the digging. Not many of the town's 34,000 residents did survive-only a few believers, and more than a few unbelievers. Wheatfield was destroyed, and at the end of that week of devil-

Induced terror the town was a broken, burned out, smoking ruin. An archaeological team (who said the devil had come to Wheatfield) came to investigate a huge stone circle, its interior barren of life. But what they were really doing was searching for a stone tablet. Satan's tablet upon which were carved these words: "He walks Amid you. The mark of the beast is plain. Believe in him once touched forever his." The kiss of life or death and the tablet had been found after that town's fall into the blackest depths of sin. Depravity had been swift, with only a few resisting the minister Alex Balloon, whose own wife was Michelle was part of the devil's team. As old and as evil as time. The Priest Father Deploy had driven a stake into her heart, and then stood by the bed with Alex Balloon, watching her metamorphosis through centuries of evil, and finally her death. The old priest was killed a short time later then the horror unfolded in Fork County. The undead walking the beast of the devil, prowling. Alex Balloon had pulled together a handful of people who were true believers in the Lord God. They fought the horror with everything they could find and with every ounce of strength and faith they possessed.

Alex had acted as the right hand of God. It was a week of mind-tearing horror, and days and nights of fear of seeking out and killing those who worship the devil, finally to save the few friends that he had, and Jane. Alex decided to make the ultimate sacrifice. He decided to fight off the advances of the Roma, the Mephistopheles witch. Roma was a beautiful woman who had given her soul to the Prince of Filth centuries before in return for everlasting youth. Alex had sent the warlock Tom Jones tumbling back to hell with a stake through his heart. All part of the bargain, then the witch Roma took Alex into the spinning darkness of trackless time, and the man of God and the witch of hell fought for Alex's seed of life. In the end, Roma beat him. Balloon was killed a short time later, and his naked body was found by the survivors, cut into pieces. The hole where his heart had been was this message tag on it

The Devil came and stood besides Alex Balloon's body. He met me and I do respect courage.

It was signed by Satan. The young doctor Tony Wood decided to raise the child that was called Sam, as his. The child would not learn the true fate of what happened to his fathers for years to come. You're late getting home," the woman had a flatness to her voice as if she knew the reason for his tardiness.

"Very difficult labor," the man lied. Jane Jones smiled ruefully but kept her thoughts to herself. "Is that a letter from Sam?" Dr. Tony Jones asked his wife. He really did not give a damn but anything was better than having to listen to her run her mouth, asking endless questions and not believing anything that he had to say.

She said, "I haven't opened it yet."

Tony laughed, "Why the hell not?" His laugher infuriated her. She rose from her chair, walking to the corner table.

"Let me show you something Tony," a bible rested on the table. Alex Balloon's bible, the Alex who was her son's true father-the son who did not yet know how or why his real father had died. But that time of unawareness was rapidly coming to a close. Jane said when Sam's letter came there was another letter also, but as she was getting ready to opened it the phone rang. Oh, fuck!

Tony thought, "Who in the hell cares?" He held up a hand, "Wait a minute. Baby, I may sense this is going to take half the night. It's been a long day and I'm beat. Let me fix you a drink baby."

"You know I don't drink, but you go ahead and fix yourself a strong one." She could smell the odor of sex on his clothing and wondered which female he had serviced this time. At that moment she realized that she hated her husband. Maybe hate is too strong of a word. Rather she loathes what he has become.

"Thanks allot." Tony walked to the wet bar fixing a strong drink. "Go on with your story," he said, "but god-damn it keep it short."

"I'll skip the details since I realize you aren't particularly interested in them and not much of anything else that lives in this house. The letter won't stay on the bible, or on the bookcase level with the bible." She did not tell him that she had called Wayne earlier, telling him about it first. Tony looked at the bible. How he hated that book; he didn't like to get too close to the offensive book. But he took the letter from his wife's hands and placed it on the bible. It flipped off onto the floor. Tony took a large gulp of his drink and again took the letter, placing it back on the bible. Again the letter was propelled off the Word of God. No matter where Tony placed the letter on a level with the bible it would not stay. He silently rejoiced, keeping his face passive. He had an idea what was happening and thought Jane did, too. She was beginning to suspect. Outside, the wind picked up in strength, tossing bits of rock and twigs against the house. The hot wind seemed almost to be a signal. Tony placed the letter under the front cover of the bible. The table began to shake as the bible and letter fell to the floor. Jane picked up the bible and placed it on the shelf. Tony grabbed the letter, looked at it, and then shook his head. When he spoke his voice was full of shock and awe, and something else Jane could not understand.

"God-damn!" Tony swore. Reverend Alex Balloon had written his name in that bible in the late forties. But such pressure had been placed on the letter that the name Alex Balloon was now clearly visible upon the white of the envelope. Tony quickly placed the letter on a low coffee table. Jane was watching closely. She thought she could see pleasure in his eyes, and something else-evil. "Impossible," Tony said, unless his words trailed off as he realized that the Master of Darkness was truly coming. Perhaps he was

All ready here! He had to get to Jean Zen. He had to tell the coven leader of this. She would be pleased at his astuteness, and perhaps reward him with some nice young girl.

"Unless what, Tony?" His wife's hated voice brought him back to his surroundings. He glanced at her face to see her face was pale, eyes calm, hands clenched into fist at her side.

"Nothing," he said.

"Well, I think Alex is trying to tell us something."

"Oh, shit! Alex is dead, Jane, more than thirty years now." Tony hoped Balloon wasn't trying to tell anybody anything.

"As we knew him, yes, he is dead. But his soul is alive. We're mortals Tony. We don't know what is behind the veil, and remember, Alex was touched by him, chosen by him if you will."

"I don't believe in that crap any more," he said, the words tumbling hatefully from his mouth. And Jane's worst suspicions were now corroborated. She wanted to slap her husband. His mood shifted as he kissed her and found it cool to his lips, very unresponsive.

"Honey, we're the youngest of the survivors of that incident and we're not kids." She pushed him away from her, his body odor was awful. She could not remember the last time Tony had showered, more evidence against him. She walked swiftly from the room, returning in a moment with an 8x10 photo of the late Alex Balloon, the picture in the frame with a glass front. Toni's eyes narrowed at the sight of the minister. He hated that bastard. He reached out to take the picture from her. "No!" She spun away from his hand.

"You think your precious Alex Balloon is some kind of fucking saint? That he's sending you messages? Hell, baby, maybe he wants some pussy."

"Pick up the letter!" She said, speaking through gritted teeth. For some reason, unexplained in his mind, Tony was suddenly afraid of his wife. He picked up the letter without questioning her. "Hold it against the glass," she said, lifting the frame photograph. There was a knowing smile on her lips that angered the man. Tony pressed the letter from his hands before the smoke turned into a blaze. The front of the envelope was slightly charred. She looked up at her husband, a smile on her lips. "Yes, Tony, I believe Alex is trying to tell me something. What's the matter darling? You seem afraid."

On Friday night the chanting would begin as no more than a low murmur in the hot night, and then grow as the winds picked up in heat and velocity. The chanting would become as profane as it was evil. The particular in the macabre chanting would gather around a huge stone. Two figures were depicted-a saintly looking man and a beastly man-creature with hooves feet. The creature and the saint have been in silent combat with no apparent winner. This area was known as the digging, the ruin of equipment and rusting old mobile homes still evident. The entire area is enclosed within a tall chain link fence. Roads to the area were destroyed in the fall of '52. Only in the last few years have they been quietly reopened by some local people. The state bought the land and condemned it because of the dangerous caves in the area, or so they said. This was the area where, for centuries, sightings of monsters have been reported-hairy, ugly beasts with red eyes and huge clawed hands and large yellow dripping fangs. All nonsense, of course. Suddenly the chanting would cease. The silence would grow heavy. The wind ceased its hot push and screaming would begin. The agonizing wailing pushing past lips, tearing out from a human whose skin was being slowly ripped from its body that was ever thought of by de Sade in his blackest moments. The shrieking would continue for hours, the torches of the now silent witness to evil flickering in the night, turning the blood-stained altar dripping a slippery black. The screaming would gradually change into a madness induced moan. Then one by one the torches would cease their flickering fiery quiver, and the area known as the digging would become as black as the devil's heart, and as still as a musty grave.

Chapter 1

Dear Mom, and Dad,

The sand and hill are a change from where I grew up, but I love it up here at Nelson College, and guess what, I'm rooming with a guy name Tom Weber Bleeder .

He's called Bleeder, has a really super fine sister who is going to a school at Harrington College, which is just upriver from us. Tom is to fix me up with her soon, said he told her all about me, says she is eager to meet me. I do wonder what her name is but I guess I'll have to wait until I meet her.

By the way, I 'm going home with them over the thanksgiving holiday to meet his parents. They live up in Canada, right on the edge of the park, beautiful land. Tom said its miles from any neighbors. I 'm really looking forward to it. Tom and I have allot in common-we both spent three years in the military.

He was in some Nebraska Canadian outfit, paratroop commando, and of course you all remember me, ranger Sam. Tom and I have done some skydiving together and we've talked about a long camp-out this spring. Maybe his good-looking sister will go along to keep me warm? I was just joking mom. Got to go, will call you later.

Love, Sam

Tony stood up, "Very interesting letter. I have to go, Jane."

"I want to know who this Tom fellow is," Jane said. "And I'd like to more about his sister."

"I'm not going to argue with you Jane, I don't give a damn what you do." "I've realized that for a amount of years, Tony. What did you mean about us being the youngest survivors?" He shrugged, "Well, Bart and

Betty, and Wayne Anita are in their sixties, all have retired, neither of them are in good

Health, and for the last few weeks neither Wayne nor Bart has acted friendly

Toward me."

"Since the hot wind began blowing?"

"Yeah, If you have to connect it that way."

Across town a phone rang, Wayne Thomas quickly silenced the jangling.

"All right, Betty, I may come right away. I know, I'll be careful. Bart wants to build a golem. What The hell is a golem? Are you serious? Okay, I'll be right over." He hung up, his face holding an odd look.

"What is wrong with Bart?" Anita asked.

"Betty says he's cracked, says the old mummer's nuts have no idea but I'll bet you it isn't complimentary."

"Well, what's a golem?"

"Ah, well, Betty says it's kind of a monster Made of clay, endowed with life. A protector, sort of." The man and wife exchanged glances. Anita shrugged.

"Wayne," she said firmly, "I don't believe its happening. Not again. I will not leave our home."

"It is happening, Anita and you know it."

"We will leave the main highway at St. Gravis," Tom said, "then we will drive northeast until we come to where mother owns some property. We'll pick up a four-wheeler, it may get rough." Sam nodded, not really paying much attention to the words of his friend and soon to be host. Since the moment he and Tom had picked up Nadia, Sam had sat in a near state of shock, overwhelmed by her beauty. He did not believe he had ever seen a more beautiful woman, and when she told him she did not have a boyfriend and that really she hardly dated at all, Sam began counting his lucky stars. Nadia was 5'6" inches tall, she told him she did not volunteer her weight, and Sam tactfully did not ask. But whatever her weight, it was distributed in the most delightful manner. Her hair was black as the darkest night, her eyes were dark brown, and her skin was flawless with just a hint of the long-ago Mediterranean ancestry. Her designer jeans were filled out perfectly. Sam could only guess at her shapely legs and his guesses would later prove one hundred percent accurate, and her breasts were full. Nadia was as taken with Sam as he was with her looking with lowered eye lids. "Sam, tell me about your family. Are your parents still living?"

"My mother is, but my real father was killed before I was born. I never really knew exactly what happened. Mother has always kind of evaded that question whenever I brought it up, said I would know someday. But I really want to know. It kind of bugs me."

"Were you ever in the special forces Sam?"

"No. I was a ranger out in California. Real good outfit-you never hear much about Rangers any more."

"Tom was a commando," she said, but there was not one bit of pride in her voice, and Sam wondered about that.

"Yes," Sam replied, "that's a good outfit, too."

"Did you see any combat, Sam?" she asked.

"Not that I may talk about, Nadia."

"In other words," she grinned, "drop the subject?"

"That's about it," Sam agreed. The three of them laughed about that.

"Men!" she said with false disgust. "But I know more about you than you think, Sam." What she knew about him or how she had learned it, he did remember to ask, but he didn't, figuring Tom had told her. The conversation lightened, and they sang songs and told jokes and the miles seemed to fly. Three young people were having fun. And then suddenly, out of the deep timber, just at that time when night reared up to touch and altar day, the massive house came into view.

Chapter Two

Falcon House:

One could almost touch the evil that hung over the small town of Wheatfield, and one could certainly see it in the eyes of the townspeople as they moved slowly up and down the streets just as it had happen in the early '50's; the evil had approached the people slowly as a lingering sickness, sluggish in its growth, but deadly when it reached the brain or the heart. Now many in that doomed town huddled in their homes, not understanding what was happening around them. The phones would not work, their cars and trucks disabled deliberately, and they were afraid. Wheatfield never regained its population total of 57,000. Fewer than 700 men, women and children now resided in the small town; perhaps 250 people in this part of Fork County, on the ranches and the farms.

But the Master of Darkness had taken note of his mistakes in the past, and did not intend to repeat them this time; no sudden departure from the churches, let that be a very gradual thing. No open rebellion, no mysterious disappearances or suspicious deaths, closing of roads and sealing off this part of the county there was no need for that now. Of the 1500, 750 residents in this part of Fork County had been inducted into the coven of the hoofed one, which was more than enough. The Lord of the Flies felt that a handful of aging Christians could do little to halt his movement in Wheatfield, and that silly old Jew with his golem that would never be anything more than several hundred pounds of clay; immobile in a box gave the Prince of Filth several moments of high humor. His followers would have several people to test their mettle upon., an ample amount to produce days of screaming and nights of sexual depravity. Depravity being one of those Christians words of course.

The King of Evil had moved slowly this time.... no need for elaborate schemes. The old Jew and Jewess would be no problem, and the aging Newspaper man and his silly wife would meet the same fate. The doctor had been easy-the Prince of Darkness had a high time playing with the good doctor over the years, tempting him, luring him, teasing him, and then finally breaking him. But Balloon's widow mother of that boy-child who was blessed by accursed meddler in the Heavens, she was another matter. She was a very strong Christian and a prissy little thing. As a goody-goody, she had resisted all of his subtle and not so subtle advances; just couldn't shake her faith in him, she was still very attractive woman-beautiful, in fact. It would be very interesting finding her breaking point: mentally, sexually, and physically. Yes, very interesting, quite.

The Master of all things did not share the Dark One's sense of humor. And while there were limits beyond which he could not go directly in dealing with the problems of facing humankind on earth, he could take a hand indirectly, other than the ultimate warning he had given. So many years before and in his Kingdom, spanning worlds and creatures and living things as yet unknown by any one outside of the firmament, all under his never closing eyes, he brooded and signed knowing Alex Balloon had slipped out again, and also knowing he was hard-pressed to contain his personal bodyguard from following, and a smile as bright as a thousand sunrises touched the face of the Universal Life of good.

"Good lord what a house!" Sam breathed in the middle of nature's beauty...

"This quiet a pad, huh, Sam?" Tom smiled.

"But how?" Sam asked, "I mean, why here? Your parents must be really rich."

"How does one really know how rich Roma and Falcon are?" Nadia said from the back seat. Sam thought he detected just a hint of irritability in her voice; a touch of maybe this is just a bit too much, too big, and too pretentious.

"Why?"

"It was originally built, or someone began it as an inn, a hotel. They ran out of money, and that's when mother and Falcon stepped in. they had money from both sides of the family, and they retired young enough to really enjoy it. And they enjoy solitude."

"They may sure have that up here," Sam observed.

"The nearest neighbor is twenty-five miles away," Tom informed him, "two of the servants are trained paramedics in case of any medical emergencies that might arise, and the house has a huge generator and several smaller back-up units. As you see, Sam, solar energy is used to help cool and heat the home. We'll give you the grand tour later so doesn't worry. The massive house has two full floors running east and west, with another single floor rising up from the center of the home, starkly commanding the second and first floor wings beneath it."

"Your parents must employ a full-time groundskeeper," Sam said.

"Several," Tom told him, "come on." Sam met the folks.

Falcon was tall and well built, a very handsome and athletic appearing man, age indeterminable. His hair was very black with a touch of gray at the temples. It did not appear to have even been touched by dye. His handshake was firm and his smile friendly, although his eyes were so dark Sam could not tell if the friendliness touched them or not. But it was Roma who literally took Sam's breath away. He was very conscious of Nadia's eyes on him when the older woman appeared in the foyer of the great house. She was the most magnificent woman Sam had ever seen. "He has his father's eyes," Roma thought, "and his father's build, and I wonder if he has his father's cock." That was a question she intended to find out.

"Mrs. Williams," Sam said taking her offered hand.

"Roma," she corrected with a smile, her hand soft and warm in his. "I'm so very happy to have the opportunity to meet you at last. Tom has written us so much about you. But we'll have time to chat later-lots of time. We have drinks at seven and dinner is at eight o'clock, informal of course." The woman before Sam was as tall as her daughter, with the same midnight black hair and full sensuous lips. Her lipstick a slash of dark red, her skin was that of her daughter's touch with the same tint. Her figure was flawless for her age, breathtaking with full heavy breasts and under her gown, long, shapely legs. Had Sam known exactly how old the woman who was once known as Nydia the witch really was, he would have passed out on the floor. Sam was very conscious of the woman's sexual gaze. Then as abruptly as the gaze was heated, it cooled, and a smile crossed her lips.

"I have the strangest sensation, Mrs. Williams," Sam said.

"Oh?" The smile did not leave her mouth.

"I feel as if I know you, as if we've met before."

"Oh, I rather doubt it, Sam, you're such a handsome young devil," she said, laughing. "I would surely remember the event. We'll chat over drinks in a few hours. We have days to get acquainted." She turned and walked from the foyer knowing full well Sam's eyes were on her body. Roma knew many things; her mind was a walking storehouse of information-all evil.

"Brazen witch!" Nadia thought, fuming as she watched her mother parade from the room, hips slightly swaying. The contempt she felt for her mother almost boiled to the surface.

"Careful mother," Tom said, "your cant captured Alex Balloon, but it failed to conquer him, and young Sam is truly his father's son. It is not worth losing a daughter to gain another conquest."

"I know both your thoughts," Roma thrust to her son, the waves stopping Sam dead in his tracks, suspending him momentarily. "And I know my daughter has begun to hate me and I know why. He is interfering, he is breaking the rules of the game, and I will have to speak to the Master." The projections ceased. Sam shook his head,

"Boy that trip must have been more tiring than I thought. I was out of it for a few seconds. It felt strange."

"It's the excitement," Tom said, "new people, new places, kind of a strain, that's all. Come on, I'll show you where to bunk."

"Where to bunk?" Sam thought, after Tom had escorted him to his rooms it was a suite consisting of a large bedroom, a sitting room, a huge bathroom, and a large walk-in closet. Sam looked for a radio but none was to be found. T.V.? None. Come to think of it, he mused, he had seen no antenna for communication. It was almost as if they wished to be cut off from the outside as much as possible.

Turning to unpack his suitcase, Sam could not shake the feeling of foreboding that hung about him and could not understand why he should feel that way. His peripheral vision saw the doorknob turning, the door easing open. Sam tensed. Nadia called the young man and grinned, expelling air from his lungs.

"Here," Nadia said as she stepped inside, closing the door behind her, "you're really a very special guest, Sam," she smiled, aware of their being alone together. "This is the first time mother has ever let a guest stay in this wing. Especially," her dark eyes sparkled with mischief, "in the room next to mine," she pointed to a closed door on the side of the room.

Sam returned the grin, "Well, I'll have to keep my door locked."

"I might try to break it down, lusting after your body."

"In that case," Sam made great haste in digging into his jeans pocket, "let me give you the key." Laughing, they stepped closer to each other. They stood for a moment, content to look into each other's eyes. Finally, Sam said, "I certainly am glad Tom invited me up here."

"I certainly am glad you came." Something clouded her dark eyes. "Sam? Be careful in this house."

"What do you mean?"

"I don't know how to explain it, but," she bit her lower lip, "sometimes Guests are changed, sort of, in a very strange kind of way."

"Spooky."

"I've seen it happen many times over the years. Watch out." The unexpected feeling of foreboding suddenly became much more intense. Both the young people whirled when the door opened behind them. Roma stood looking at them.

"I could not help overhearing," she said. "You'll find my daughter has a very active imagination. She desires to become a fiction writer and I think she sometimes has difficulty separating fact from fiction." She held out a hand to her daughter, "Come, dear, let's not be rude and prevent our quest from taking his rest." Sam caught a flicker of something very close to contempt in Nadia's eyes.

"Of course, mother." She glanced at Sam, "See you in an hour or so. Perhaps you'd enjoy a swim before cocktails? We have an indoor pool and a selection of trunks in case Tom forgot to tell you to bring a suit."

"He did and I'd love a swim."

"I'll tap on your door in about an hour. That door." She pointed to the connecting door among their rooms, and then glared openly and defiantly at her mother. The women left, with Roma closing the door, flashing a brief smile at Sam. A smile that left Sam guessing at its true content.

Sam, like his father, although not to the degree of the elder Balloon, was worldly and he thought he stretched out on the bed and was asleep in three minutes-the deep sleep of a young person at the very pinnacle of health and physical conditioning. He dreamed of a strange looking medallion but could not bring the relief of the medal into clear focus. In his dream Sam questioned where he had seen the medallion. Then it came to him-around the necks of Tom and his mother, some sort of family crest, he imagined. And he pushed the dream from his mind and slept. As he slept, the cross around his neck, the cross that had belonged to his father, began to glow in the darkness of the room. It seemed to pulse with life.

Chapter Three

Roma and Nadia in bikinis were just about more than Sam could take Several times the young man had to hit the water of the pool to cool off his emotion, throttling an uncomfortable stiffness. Roma had to be in her mid to late fifties, but she had the body of a twenty year old without any sign of aging, no sagging, no marks anywhere on her body to show her real age. She was absolute sheer flawless, physical perfection, and Sam's eyes greedily drank in their beauty whenever he felt it was safe to look without being obvious. Although several times he got the impression they were both parading for his benefit. Neither Tom nor Falcon were poolside and Sam asked Roma about that while Nadia lapped the pool.

"Oh, they're discussing some financial matters, I 'm sure," she said, smiling unearthly. "As far as I'm concerned, neither of them care for swimming. They prefer riding or fencing. Both are quite good with the rapier. Do you fence, Sam?"

"No, ma'am." She laughed,

"Ma'am? Really, Sam, that makes me feels positively ancient. "Roma, please." She cut her eyes and visually traveled over the young man's body, lingering at his crotch. "Yes," she thought, "just like his father, amply endowed." Sam felt he was being mentally raped. He was.

Sam cleared his throat. "May I ask a personal question, Roma?"

"You may ask anything you wish, Sam."

"Okay, lady," he thought, "how about you and me finding the nearest bed and get it on?" Then he was aware of a burning sensation in the center of his chest right where his cross usually lay.

Roma smiled. " I'm flattered, Sam. its quite nice that a handsome young man, certainly young enough to be my son would desire me."

"You're not angry with me for thinking that?" Again, there was that strange burning sensation in the center of his chest.

"Don't be silly. I can't imagine a woman who would be angry with you

Thinking that."

"How do you do that? I mean, read people's minds?"

"Was that the personal question you were going to ask?"

"No, ma'am, I mean, Roma."

"You were going to ask how I managed to stay so young-looking."

"Damn," he muttered, "I 'm really going to have to control my thoughts."

"I was born in Rumania, Sam, well, a few years ago," she laughed. "I have a mixture of racing in me, and my mother was astonishingly beautiful. My mother, Roma Christian Nadia, was well over two-hundred years old when she died, and still quite attractive." Her face took on a serious look. "She died begging for her life while Lilith the witch bludgeoned her to death, laughing as she did. So I really take no special care of my body other than to exercise daily and watch my diet." With that she rose from the poolside lounger and executed a clean, graceful dive into the water just as her daughter was walking toward them, rubbing her hair with a thick towel. Sam watched her stride toward him; like her mother, ripe perfection and like dressed in a bikini that scarcely covered all the essentials.

"My mother is quite a woman, isn't she?" Nadia asked, sitting down and catching her breath from her laps in the heated water.

"At least that, Nadia. I would think Falcon would be extremely jealous of her."

"Did she come on to you, Sam? Sure she did," she said, not giving him time to answer the question. "Oh, they both do what they want to do. They have their little affairs. I've known about them both for years."

"Why do I get the feeling you and your mother don't get along?"

"Because it's true. We're civil to each other most of the time but us Stopped being friends a long time ago."

"Care to talk about it?"

"Later. Here comes the never aging sexpot." Sam shook his head at the acid in Nadia's remark.

"Nadia has been going to church," Tom said to Falcon. The men sat in the study, the heavy doors closed.

"I know it, so Roma is noting what we may do about it for several reasons but we know he has been meddling."

"But, why? I thought the rules he follows," Falcon cut him off with a wave of his hand - a curt slash of impatience.

"The master makes the rules, each knowing they may break them at will, if really, any rules do exist, which I more and more doubt. But nevertheless, we are required to follow what our individual master dictates. And, don't ask questions. What goes on in the minds of the two supreme beings is beyond the grasp of even us. When are the others arriving?"

"Tomorrow at 11:00 a.m. I have arranged for a plan to bring them in."

"Does the Balloon bastard know of their coming?"

"No. Neither does Nadia." Falcon brooded for a time, his dark features unreadable. "You feel how many to be ready converts?"

"Five young men-six young women and the three for our own entertainment. Leave the men for Roma, we'll share the women."

"Are them young and tender? Lovely? Virgins?"

"I think... possibly three. Linda is curious of our Master, so she will be easy to convert, an easier fuck, but one of them I know is pure. She is the one I picked for you." Both men laughed the chuckling of evil.

"Problems should they vanish?"

"By the time they are missed it will be all ready too late, and everything will be over and done with. Balloon bastard is to be Roma's exclusively. You understand that?"

"Yes, Falcon."

"Unless she tells me differently, you may have to kill your sister, Tom, or on a more pleasant note, plant your seed within her. Does either prospect disturb you?" The young warlock shrugged his reply.

"Good, you are your mother's child. Well now, a full ten days." He smiled the smile as corrupt as his heart was dark. I am looking forward to the time.

The hot wind picked up, rousing Jane from a fitful sleep. Tony had not returned. She opened her eyes and gasped in fright when she saw the mist began to change to take some shape and her fright turned into a mixture of relief and joy. Jane smiled.

"I will do what I may to help," the voice said, beating a silent message inside her head. "But I don't know how much he will allow me to do. I am rather a maverick within the kingdom."

"Oh, Alex!"

"Let me finish. You have lost half of all you once loved. Balloon flung his message and I may tell you no more than that. Help Bart and Wayne while you may. In the end, it will be up to you and the clay man, but more weight will be put on your shoulders, your faith." She did not understand.

"Tony, he is the half I have lost?"

"I may tell you no more now." Jane knew then that her suspicions had been correct. Tony had gone to the other side.

"Our son?" "He will be tempted and he will fall from grace more than once during the next ten days. But I may do little to help. I will attempt to see him. I think he will be finding an unexpected ally coming forward but my place is with you, and at the end you will have a choice to make." And Jane knew what that choice would be. "Don't be too hasty in your decision." Balloon hurled the Warning. "You have many, many good years ahead of you, and you don't have to do this. Once you have decided, the only alternate is to accept the Dark One's offer."

"I will never do that. I love you, Alex. I want to be with you."

"I must go now," Balloon projected, "be careful." The mist began to disperse, becoming shapeless, formless, then one slim tentacle of mist broke from the vapor and moved down the side of the bed to touch Jane on her cheek. When the mist was gone, she put her hand to her cheek and the spot was damp. Soon her tears had kissed the touch of love that endured...... of life after death.

Dinner had been quite an event, the setting something Sam had witnessed only in the movies. The meal had been served in courses, and the coffee was the best he had ever tasted.

"Mother owns the lands in Columbia," Tom explains, "we have the beans flown in and grind them ourselves." Falcon was very polite throughout the meal, but not given to much conversation, he and Tom excused themselves after dinner and went into the study, closing the door. Nadia said she was going to bed and would see him in the morning. The look fired at Sam was a warning and Sam did not really understand it-at least he tried to convince himself of that. Roma rose from her chair and held out her hand.

"Come, Sam, walk with me. The night air will do us good." He held her wrap and was conscious of the heady perfume wafting into his nostrils. He was grateful when they stepped out into the cold night air of the terrace. "Tell me about you, Sam," she said, standing very close to him.

"Not that much to tell. I'm twenty two-years old, went right into the army right after high school, did my time, and glad I did. Here I am."

"You and Tom and Nadia were born in '59."

"Where were they born, Roma?"

"Rumania."

"I thought that county was under communist control."

"I traveled wherever I chose, Sam. My investments are worldwide.

Tell me about your father."

"I never knew him. He died before I was born. My mother married a doctor before I was born. He delivered me. Doctor Jones."

"But you all ready knew this Jones person was not your father?"

"Oh, yes. They made that clear when I was old enough to understand. My dad was a minister."

"In more ways than one," she thought. "But you never had the calling?"

"Me?" Sam laughed. "Oh, no, but I have worn dad's cross around my neck all my life." He touched the center of his chest, feeling the outline of the cross. The witch Roma fought to keep herself from recoiling away from the young man. She remembered that cross very well. It had burned her several times while she and Alex Balloon fought in the circles through timeless space, neutral ground, ruled by no master. Roma shivered.

"Cold?" Sam touched her arm instinctively, protectively at the touch. His chest began that strange burning, now much more intense.

"No," she said shortly. The mention of that damned cross driving all thoughts of sex from her. She moved away from his touch; the burning in the center of his chest ceased. "I must go." She moved toward the house. "I'll see you in the morning, Sam. Sleep well." She was gone, the darkness of her gown fading into the night. Footsteps echoed on the stone walkway leading from the yard. Sam turned. A tall, almost emaciated-looking man slowly made his way up to the terrace.

"Best you go in the house now, sir." The man spoke slowly as if the act of speaking was painful.

"Why?"

"Because it is going to rain, and you are not dressed for the elements." Sam looked up into the sky. Thousands of stars twinkled down at him.

"But there isn't a cloud in the sky!"

"It will rain," the man insisted, "soon."

"What's your name?" Sam asked.

"Johnson David."

"Have you worked for the Williams long?"

"Years. Go in the house now." He turned, and the night seemed to dissolve him. Sam listened for the sound of fading footsteps, but none could be heard. The man appeared to have vanished.

"Johnson?"

Sam thought. "Now where have I heard that name before?" He was lying in his bed, conscious of Nadia in the next room. Near, but so far. Just before sleep spread its gentle blanket over him, Sam was still musing over the tall man with the somehow familiar name. And on the dresser, the cross glowed dully.

"Meddling!" Satan fired a dirty salvo into the heavens. "Always meddling. Why can't you abide by the rules?"

"You are complaining about rules being broken Amadeus?"

"How roll. We made an agreement eons ago. You rule the heavens and I rule the earth."

"I don't recall any hard and fast set of rules." The master of all chuckled and the heavens rumbled with thunder.

"Hoofed one, you bemuse me. Your mind, hat there is of it is open for inspection. maverick resident returned to earth by his own volition, not with my permission. You lifted the veil which was not necessary. Balloon is a curious one, and a brave one. He takes chances, he pries, he investigates. Besides, he boundaries that divide life from death are at best, a dowdy and vague. Who shall say where the one ends and the other begins?" Satan howled his laughter, foulness stinking up the air.

"That s not very original of you, thunder breath. Have you taken to spend your time reading Poe?"

"Idiot! Who do you suppose put the thought in his mind?"

"I was under the impression it was I. That says a great deal for your Intelligence. I don't have to stand here and be insulated."

"Anywhere you go is an insult to someone."

"Bah!" and the heavens became silent as a gentle rain began falling over Falcon's house and the grounds surrounding it.

Chapter Four

"Bart!" the mist formed at the foot of the Jew's bed. "Open your eyes and look at me." Bart fearfully opened his eyes looking at the mist. He began silently reciting prayers, recalling them as if he had just stepped out of the synagogue. Bart tried to speak but found he was voiceless. "Don't be alarmed." The mist thrust its silent projection as it began to take on a shape. "I may hear your thoughts."

"Go away!" Bart said. "Alex? My God! Oh I think I'm having a heart attack.

"And I think you're as full of it now as when I knew you years ago."

"Don't think," ugly Bart sat up in bed, "you're too close to him to take chances."

"Bart?" Betty stirred by his side. "What's wrong?"

"I should tell you and you'd have an accident in your gown." "Nothing," his voice popped from his throat, "a little gas is all."

"Umm," she said, and then fell into a deep sleep.

"She won't wake up again until I leave," Alex projected. "You may speak normally."

"I wish you had taught me how to do that year ago."

"I didn't know years ago."

"Alex, I'm dreaming all this, right?"

"It is not a dream."

"I was afraid you'd say that. Alex, I 'm an old man with more than my share of aches and pains-bad circulation and that other thing, too. Arteriosclerosis and I got..."

"Not any more, Bart."

"What do you mean Alex?"

"Do your legs hurt you, Bart?" Bart thought about that for a moment, his hands feeling his thin legs. They were not cold, nor did they ache. He looked at the mist and said,

"What did you do Alex?"

"Corrected a few physical problems that you and Wayne will have to be strong mentally and physically, to make it through this upcoming ordeal."

"Why am I experiencing this feeling that I am about to get the shitty excuse me, Alex, end of this handle?"

"I don't speak Hebrew."

"Bargain you really don't? That seems odd-all languages are as one there."

"Bart? Bart? Am I your friend?"

"Oh, here it comes now. I knew it."

"Wouldn't you rather go out in a blaze of glory, Bart?"

"If it's all the same to you, I rather not go out at all, Do you realize what you're doing to me? You turned my head all cockeyed more than twenty years ago. I 'm a Jew and I don't believe in all this crazy stuff. Now here you come again. No offense meant Alex, please. It's good to see you, what there is of you to see. But old Alex, what do you want from this old man? Let me rephrase that-what's going to happen to me?"

"You're going to meet the man in ten days."

"Some friend you are! You fix my legs all up to where they don't hurt first time in five years, then you tell me I'm going to die in ten days." He lay back on the pillow and he closed his eyes. "If I don't see you and don't talk to you, you'll go away." He was still for a few moments until curiosity got the best of him. He opened his eyes and the mist that was Alex Balloon was still there looking at him. Bart sighed, then said, "Well, sometimes it works okay Alex... I never could win an argument with you. What do you want me to do?"

"Finish the clay man."

"I knew that was coming, too."

"I will speak to Wayne and Anita. Perhaps Wayne, only. They will come to stay with you and Betty. The clay man will have powers for ten days only for the duration of the siege. When life leaves him the four of you will go home."

"How is it, Alex? I mean, where you stay?"

"Different, but I don't stay there often. I 'm usually in trouble with him I believe."

"Alex? What does this make me? This flies in the face of all that I was taught as a child. Everything I was taught to believe."

"I cannot say what it makes you. That will be your choice at the end."

"Wonderful," Bart said dryly, "I love a mystery." The mist began to fade.

"Alex!" Bart cried. "What about Jane?" The mist projected its reply and Bart was saddened.

Breakfast at the mansion was served buffet style with Sam and Nadia eating together. "Did you sleep well?" she asked.

"Passed out," Sam said, buttering a piece of bread. "I don't recall ever sleeping so soundly in my life."

"It's the silence in the woods but sometimes it may be well, frightening."

"How?" Her eyes were serious as they fixed their beauty on Sam's face.

"Do you believe in the Devil, Sam?"

"Of course."

"Do you believe in possession?" Sam chewed thoughtfully for a few seconds.

"Yes, I do, Nadia, even though most Protestants don't, but my father did. My real father, mother told me, he did. My stepfather was raised in the Catholic church but he broke from it when I was about eleven years old-just a kid. Tony stopped worshiping God-just quit. I don't know what happened but mother taught me the bible and to believe in demonic possession. One thing she stressed was that the Devil walks the earth. Yeah, it was about that time I started hearing whispers about Tony running around on mother, but," he shrugged, "his loss. Mother is beautiful. I don't understand men who run Around on their wives. Sorry, I 'm digressing. Why do you ask about possession?"

"Are you a Christian, Sam?"

"Well, technically yes, I suppose I am. I'm not very pure at heart at times, though."

"Christians aren't supposed to be perfectly pure. I don't believe that's possible for a human."

"Sounds like you're really serious about religion, Nadia. I mean, don't take that the wrong way, so am I. It's serious business and I would like to know more about it, yes."

"Tell me Sam, may you still be a Christian and lust after someone?"

"I don't think, Nadia."

"That's a human trait, isn't it? Yes, I think you may if you recognize the fault and try to do something about it. I think being a Christian means believing in god, trying to do the right by his commandments. I think it all depends on how a person lives his or her total life; do you help others in need? Try to think good thoughts? Do the best you may? Those types of things." He smiled.

"Are you lusting after someone Nadia?"

"Yes," she put her hand on his and squeezed gently. Sam returned the gentle caress.

"I couldn't take my eyes off you after we met."

"I felt the same way, and Sam? It's funny sort of. I got the feeling that it was right. You know what I mean?"

"Yes. It was…odd. I have never felt anything like it. You know, we're going to have to be careful. Your mother reads thoughts."

"What do you mean Sam?" He told her of the events at poolside, her expression was one of confusion.

"I wonder why she kept that from me all these years?" She shyly rubbed her fingertips on the back of his hand. "Roma is also lusting after you, Sam, and she'll have you, Sam." He shook his head. "Yes, she will. Roma always gets what she wants, one way or another. Don't anger her, Sam, please. I 'm afraid of her and I always have been. I May's say more-not until I'm certain of the thoughts in my mind. Thanks, brother," Nadia said, fire flickering in her eyes.

"A couple of those you named are okay, the rest are creeps. I cannot tolerate them. That's the problem, brother dear. I do know them. I'll get the cook to pack us a lunch, Sam. Let's go as quickly as possible." She whirled and left the room, her anger evident in her step.

"You and sis have plans for today, Sam?"

"Hiking, exploring some."

"Be careful, and don't get lost," Tom cautioned with a grin. "It's pretty wild out there."

"Oh, I'll be careful, Tom. Like you, I've had some pretty extensive training in staying alive."

The young men locked glances, Tom finally saying, "Yes, that's true. I've often wondered just which one of us is the tougher." Sam's smile was tight.

"I hope you never have to find out, Tom." Sam left it at that.

Sam had more of his father in him than even his mother suspected, for he never traveled unprepared. In his rooms, after dressing in jeans, a heavy shirt, and jump boots, Sam slid a heavy bladed knife in his leather sheath, onto his belt, and he had brought with him, quite illegally, a snub nosed .38 pistol. He slipped that into the pocket of his jacket and then knocked on Nadia's door. "You ready, Nadia?" The door opened and she stood before him-a young lady just as beautiful in jeans and rough shirt as in a ballroom gown. "You look good enough to eat," Sam told her.

"I've thought about that, too," she said, a smile on her lips. Sam cleared his throat and decided to shift gears and head in another direction.

"Nadia? Why don't you like those people Tom invited up here?"

"You don't know?" She seemed surprised. "I guess not. They have a cult at Nelson College. They have tried several times to get me to join. I refused."

"What kind of cult?"

"They practice Devil Worshiping." Sam did not realize just how isolated they were until he and Nadia got into the deep timber on the edge of the big park just south of the Williams' home. The dark timber closed around them about 500 meters from the edge of the estate.

"Beautiful," Sam said, "so beautiful and peaceful." Nadia started to reply when three shots cut through the crisp air. Sam instinctively grabbed for the pistol in his coat, checking his movement just before touching the inner pocket. Nadia caught the quick movement and smiled.

"It's a signal to return to Falcon house," she said. "Come on. It might be important."

"Sir," Johnson said, "There was a radio message for you just moments after you left. In the communication room Mr. Falcon is waiting. The message is rather tense, Sam." Falcon handed him a slip of paper. "I do hope this will not altar your plans to visit with us." Sam did not reply until he had read the message.

Montreal flight 128# 1634–58JA. He looked into Falcon's dark unreadable eyes. "This is it?"

"That was the entire message, Sam. I asked for a repeat, and that was it."

"Well, I guess I have to get to Montreal somehow."

"We'll take the Rover," Nadia said. "We'll go together."

"Now," dear Roma opened her mouth to protest. Daughter met mother, head to head with an unwavering look.

"I know the roads, mother. Sam doesn't, so I 'm going with him." There was firmness to her voice that said she would book no more objections.

Roma smiled, "Of course, dear. I was only going to suggest you change into something more suitable for the trip."

"Certainly you were," just short of condescending, "but we'll go as we are. Come on, Sam." She pulled at his arms. "We'll be there in a few hours."

"JA?"

"My mother's initials." Nadia shuddered besides him.

"Cold?" Sam asked.

"No," suddenly frightened for some reason. "I just got the worst feeling of….I don't know, foreboding, I guess I'd call it."

"Nadia?" She glanced at him. "I have a feeling."

Flight 128# came in and emptied its load of passengers. Sam knew no one on the flight. Sam and Nadia sat in the now deserted arrival area looking at each other with questions unspoken in their eyes.

"Son?" The disembodied sounding voice came from behind the young couple. Sam was conscious of a burning sensation in the center of his chest. They turned, looking, no one was in sight. Nadia dug nervous fingers into Sam's forearm.

"Son? Was that what that voice said?"

"Easy now," Sam attempted to calm her. His own nerves were rattled.

"Sam?" she said. "Look on the table in front of us." Sam slowly, almost reluctantly pulled his gaze to the front. A manila envelope lay on the low table. "That wasn't there a second ago."

"I know." Again, they looked around them. The arrival area and the corridor were deserted. They both stared at the envelope. Sam touched the packet. It was cold to the touch. He picked it up and carefully opened it. There was a picture and several sheets of paper. The picture was of his father.

Sam looked at the 8x10 for a long moment, and then handed it to Nadia. "My dad." His words were charged with emotion, spoken in a husky tone.

"I may see where you got your good looks," she said. "He was a rugged handsome man. Sam? Who put the envelope on the table? And who was that who spoke to you? And where did he go? Sam, there was no one within shouting distance." There was a slight grimace of pain on Sam's face. "Sam?"

"I don't know the answer to any of those questions, Nadia, but I'll tell you this-when that voice spoke, my chest started burning. It's just now going away, but man, did it hurt for a few seconds."

"Your chest?"

"The skin on my chest. Right in the center." He looked around them. No one was in sight. Sam unbuttoned his shirt. Hearing Nadia's gasp as his t-shirt came into view, "Relax, I 'm not going to strip." He tried to grin. "At least not here."

"That's not it Sam," she said, her voice tiny. "Look at your t-shirt; the center of your chest." He looked down and the fabric was burned brown in the shape of a cross, the cross Sam wore. His father's cross. Nadia reached out. Pulling up his t-shirt the cross had burned in his skin, leaving a scar in the shape of a cross. Sam touched the red scar. It was no longer painful even though he could see it was burned deeply. Sam unfolded the pages and almost became physically ill. The handwriting was unmistakably his father's scrawl. Sam had seen it many times on old sermons.

"Sam? You're as white as a ghost!"

"I think that's what just spoke to me. My father wrote this." The young man wiped his suddenly blurry eye and once more looked at the writing, reading slowly, and Nadia silently reading with him.

"Son writing is difficult for me, in my condition. Want to keep this as brief as possible but yet there are so many things I must say to you and the girl."

"How?" Nadia said, then shook her head, not believing any of this.

"I have watched you, son, whenever possible, grow through the years. Tried to guide you, help you as best I could. Nadia, too. The girl besides you, not the Nydia I knew. Like that time you got drunk in your mother's car and passed out at the wheel. That was a close one, boy. I'm the only person in the world who knew about that, Sam."

"Sam," Nadia said, "in this world," is wondering why she said that.

"Give the cross you have around your neck to the girl. Do it, son, without delay, time is of the essence." Sam removed the cross from his neck and handed it to Nadia.

"Put it on," he said. He could see she was, for some reason softly crying. "No one will be able to remove that cross from her. No one. I cannot guarantee she will not be hurt, but well, you must have faith. Now then, a cruel blow for each of you, for I know your thoughts. Nadia is your half sister."

"Oh, my God!" she said.

"When I knew her mother, Roma was not her name. Her name was Nydia. She is of and for the Devil. She is a witch after the hooded one….. Attempted to take over the town of Wheatfield and failed then, during which Wayne and Anita, Tony, Jane, Betty, Bart and myself killed hundreds of coven members. I made a bargain with God to save your mother and what few Christians I won, in a sense, but so did the woman you know as Roma. I killed or at least thought I sent Tom Weber back to hell. Tom is your brother; he is a representative for Satan-a warlock. When you leave this terminal the both of you must go to a catholic church, get as much holy water as you may for you will need it. I must rest for a moment. Writing is not something one does where I reside." Sam glanced at Nadia.

"Half sister?" She met his eyes. Read his thoughts I don't care, Sam shook his head in confusion and returned to the letter.

"It would be wrong, son, to say the Devil is back for he never leaves the earth; so I'll simply say he has returned to Wheatfield. There will soon be a great tragedy in Wheatfield and I'll be there to help your mother for her ordeal involves both of us…… and the girl. There will be no survivors from Wheatfield This time. None."

"Mother?" Sam whispered.

And as if Balloon had anticipated the question, the letter continued, "She had made her choice. Tony has gone over to the other side. He has done so willingly; indeed a long time ago. I could not stop him, for his faith is weak, as his flesh. And that is something you will have to deal with as well. You have a mission, Sam, and I do not envy you your task, for it may destroy you. Not necessarily physically, and I may say no more about that. But you will be tempted, and you will fall to some of those temptations, for you are a mortal, blessed in a manner of speaking, but still a mortal. A coven is being established at Falcon, it is a house of evil, and you must return there. Your job is there. You will not be able to contact any one in Wheatfield. Wheatfield is dead, past saving, but your mother will speak to you in some way before she slips through the painful darkness to the other side and to peace and blue light. We will meet someday, son, I am certain of that, and may tell you no more about my surety. The feelings you and the girl share is something that you both must cope with. I cannot help you, and will not lecture you. But I will say this: the union that produced Nadia was not a holy union. If anything, it was blessed by The Dark One."

"Riddles," Sam said. "The letter is filled with riddles, and I don't know what they mean."

"I love you deeply, Sam, and wish I could be of more help to you in your task, but I have said too much all ready. , I must go. Place the picture of me in the envelope for that is all of me I may give you that will remain tangible. Put the letter on the table and do not touch it again.

Love, your Father"

Sam placed the picture in the envelope and the letter on the table. Together still in mild shock, not knowing what to believe, the young man and woman Watched the pages dissolve into nothing. Then they were alone. Nadia put her head on Sam's shoulder and wept.

"I have done all I may do to help Sam," said the silent voice as it pushed out of the mist and into the sleeping brain of Jane. She sat up on the couch, rubbing her eyes.

"When did you see Sam?"

"About a minute ago, in Montreal."

"Neat trick, since you're in front of me at this moment. I won't pursue how you managed that."

"That would be best. You will understand soon enough."

"A time warp?"

"There is no time in my world. A year is the blink of an eye. Drop it Jane."

"All right." She stared hard at the misty face of the only man she had ever loved.

"Tell me this, how did our son look?"

"Considering the circumstances, well and confused, upset." The misty face smiled, then projected, "Bewitched, bothered, and bewitched"

"Oh, Alex!"

"Now you see why he is constantly calling me on the carpet, so to speak. Our son is falling deeply in love." Jane smiled. "How wonderful with his half sister."

"You were a rounder before you came to Wheatfield, weren't you?"

"Yes, but well, I'll explain at a later date."

"I 'm not sure I want to hear about it."

"As you wish, but don't jump to conclusion." She glanced at the clock on the fireplace mantel.

"Tony might be back for lunch any moment."

"Tony will never again set foot in this house, Jane, not for any decent Purpose that is."

"I don't understand."

"You will."

"Bart?" Betty called down the basement steps, "what are you doing? I keep telling you and telling you I am building a golem, so stay out of here. No telling what this thing might get in its head."

"How may a thing with clay for brains get something into its head?"

"I don't care to argue with you." A moment of heavy silence. Bart looked up she was still standing in the doorway.

"I believe you, Bart," she said quietly.

"Oh?" his voice drifted up full of disbelief, "so what changed your mind?"

"You remember me saying you were as crazy as vents after you told me about speaking with Alex Balloon?"

"How could I forget being called a bedbug?"

"So?"

"He's in the kitchen now, so ask him to take a seat. I'll be right up."

There was no Alex in the kitchen, but Wayne was. "I cannot believe you are seriously considering taking part in this insanity."

"Honey, you didn't see Alex last night, either."

"Well honey," she mimicked him, "neither did you. I warned you about that second piece of cake."

"Babe," he was very patient with her, "we've been through allot together.

I've tried to bring you along easy as I may but now it is time to lay it down straight for you. Just take a look around you, and tell me, what do you see? Look at all of our neighbors' houses. What do you see?"

"The people sitting on the porches."

"Any of them waving at us? Any of them calling for us to stop by and have a cup of coffee or tea like we used to do?" She looked straight ahead Refusing to speak. "He's here, Betty. He's back. The Dark One. Alex says this time Wheatfield is through."

"If your friend the spirit man is all-fired up, why doesn't he just waves his hand and makes all this go away?" Tears sprang into her eyes.

"Hatefulness goes away? Did you pack like I asked you?" she sighed yes. "Bart, I'll humor you until we may get into a mental hospital."

"Betty old girl," he spoke softly, "my wife of so many good years listens to me. We're not going to make it out of this. We're going to die, and Alex says the only thing he may do is make it as easy as possible."

"How considerate of him." Wayne turned into the drive, parking by the corner street lamp.

"We're here, honey."

"Oh, goody!" she clapped her hands. "Do I get to see the monster now? A double treat? Ooh, I may hardly wait. This is better than the time that we went to the county fair." Wayne held her hand as they walked up the sidewalk and up the steps to the porch. Anita opened the door for them.

"Thank God!" Anita cried. "A face I know is normal and a mouth that is not raving things that go bump in the night. I'll get the luggage out of the car," Wayne said. Betty stepped into the house and stopped dead still in the living room. A giant man stood against the wall across the room. It was at least eight and a half feet tall. It was faceless. She turned to ask Anita what that thing was. Was this some kind of joke and what's the occasion for a party? She dropped her purse on the carpet as her eyes found the mist hovering just above the carpet chair.

"I believe you know the," Anita said. And she fainted.

Chapter Five

They had gone to a hardware store and brought several containers. Ten went to half a dozen catholic churches seeking holy water. The priests, once they saw the young couple were sincere, asked no question but merely gave them as much holy water as they needed. "I just don't know if my mind may accept all that's been thrown at me this day," Nadia said. "But allot of things are beginning to fall into place."

"Explain that?" Sam asked. They were halfway back to the Williams mansion, eating a mild-afternoon lunch by the side of the road; the lunch they were supposed to have eaten while exploring the woods.

"Well, this is only a small part of it Sam, but have you ever seen a home that didn't have some religious paraphernalia somewhere? A painting, a cross a bible… something? I haven't. Our house is bear of anything religious, but that could be explained away by the fact that that Roma and Falcon don't go to church. But I know what an upside down cross means and both Roma and Falcon and Tom have those in their rooms, and they always go somewhere on Friday night. They stay all night and return at dawn and they all wear the same kind of medallion.

"I 'm surprised they haven't tried to get you to join and to wear a medallion."

"Oh, they have dozens of times, beginning when I was just a small child, but it always irritated my neck; caused great ugly rashes; made me sick, very sick. The last time was just a couple years ago. Roma threw the medallion away. It was gold, Sam, worth hundreds of dollars, and she just threw it away and flew into a rage and kept saying, 'Damn that son of a bitch! Tom, you knew this was going to happen and damn that bastard preacher.' I didn't know what she was talking about, Sam, raving was more like it. And I didn't ask. Dad wrote about Tom Weber the devil's representative. The preacher must have been dad." She covered his hand with hers. "Sam? For years they've kept it from me or tried to, but they practice evil. I May's prove it, for they're very Careful, but I know they do. That house is evil, the people who work for them are evil, and David, the way he looks at me-something about him frightens me. I wish I could recall where I've seen him before." They looked up as a huge helicopter flapped and roared overhead. The helicopter cable that was carrying fourteen passengers was soon out of sight heading for the house. Nadia said glumly, "Poor Judy and the others. They don't have any idea what they're getting into."

"Judy?"

"And Betty Cloyed. Betty was a small dark haired girl and very pretty. She doesn't know what they have in store for her. Betty, Judy, Jean, Linda, Susan all of them are virgins. Come to think of it. All of them are virgins. I don't much like Linda. She is supposed to be a virgin, so the word goes. It's something I May's put my fingers on."

"Falcon likes young women?"

"Oh, yes," she quickly replied, "for a fact. I've seen him looking at me in a way that makes me uncomfortable, just like Davie."

"Have either of them ever tried anything with you?"

"Oh, no, never."

"Tell me about Falcon. You know, he isn't your real father. Has he been around long?"

"For as long as I may remember. There sin. I really don't know where they get their money-either of them. I was told they both owned interests in a amount of factories and businesses and that this is where they got their money. I do know that mother owns a company that makes wines and perfume, and another company that makes clothing for women. I've seen those businesses."

"Tell me about the people who run them, those you had chance to meet." She was again reflective for a moment.

"Yes, I see what you mean; they seemed to be afraid of Roma but yet," The sentence trailed into silence, "the medallion-the top people all wore medallions like mother and Falcon and Tom."

"And the one your mother tried to make you wear?"

"Just like it."

"And did they ever meet on a Friday? Friday seems to hold a special significance."

"Yes, several times. And it was just like I told you before; they would all disappear about dark and not return until dawn. Mother said it was business, and not to worry. I always had someone staying with me, a sitter or a companion. Sam? I'm frightened."

"I don't believe we could do anything else."

"Sam lets try. Let's see if we may just run away, go back to Washington State. Please? Let's try." Sam hesitated, not wanting to risk angering his father if any of this is real and not a dream. He wavered, sensing that Nadia's fear was very close to overwhelming her. "We'll try," he said.

But the four-wheeler would not start. Sam complained of his chest burning and the glowing ceased. "All that could be a fluke," Nadia suggested. Sam turned around, heading back to Montreal. The four-wheeler died in the middle of the road. The burning and the glowing began again. Nadia said, "All right, Mr. Balloon. No more. We'll go back." The four-wheeler started; the glowing and the burning faded.

"Any doubts now?" Sam asked. She shook her head.

"But where do we start, Sam?"

At Falcon house, "What do we do?" Anita asked. She had recovered from her shocked state and sat sipping tea, her gaze alternating among the mute, huge motionless clay man and the mist that was Balloon.

"Wait," Balloon projected.

"None of you may start it. The golem will not kill without some overt provocation towards one of you."

"What may that thing do?" Wayne asked. "It has the strength of thirty men. It cannot be stopped by anything mortal. A golem is all things of this earth. But none of you need concern yourself with the mysteries of the cosmos. The golem will have no will other than what I give it." Outside, although the day was bright and clear and warm, thunder rattled the window of the house.

"Excuse me," Balloon said, "no one will accept that which we give it." The thunder ceased. Bart said a very a quick and fervent prayer while Anita clutched at a small bible. Wayne seemed bemused. Betty looked at him and said,

"You find this bemusing?"

"He's still a reporter at heart," Alex said.

"I have personally witnessed one of the greatest stories a reporter could possibly witness, back in '57," Wayne replied, "and am about to witness another, and I am unable to write about either."

"Pity, the whole town, all of our friends has turned against us," Anita said bitterly, "and all you may think about is reporting a story."

"Our friends are dead," Wayne replied. "Just like before, they have rejected the teaching of the Almighty and of his son, Jesus Christ. They have made their choice, so be it."

"I'll go along with the almighty part," Bart said, "the bit about his son?" He waggled his hand. "I've got to see it to believe it." Alex Balloon seemed bemused by the exchange. Betty said, looking at the misty form, "He could clear it all up so we may get a look at him." Bart grinned.

"Stop it!" Anita screamed. "It isn't a joke, my god! I May's take this joking around our deaths." Wayne put an arm around her, pulling her to him.

"I think it's the best way to hide our fears, honey, but you're right, it is no joking matter."

"Everything mortals question will be explained," Balloon projected, "in time." Anita pushed her husband from her, took a deep breath, and glared at the Mist form that was once her minister.

"I believe in you with all my heart and faith. Twenty years ago, brother Balloon, and I do now."

"Good." Balloon said.

"Someone's walking up the sidewalk," Bart said. "

"Jane," Balloon projected, "I asked her to come.

"She is going to stay with us, isn't she?" Betty asked.

"No, the clay man will protect you. I will stay with Jane. You will all know why that must be at a later time."

Bart laughed, "See momma? Who says there isn't sex after life?"

"Bart!" she whirled around, glaring at him. "You shut your mouth with talk like that." Her face suddenly split into a wide grin. "Beside, for the past seven years, that's all you've been able to do."

"Talk!" Bart reddened, and then grinned. He leaned back in his chair and folded his arms across his thin chest. He had a retort but thought it best to keep it to him.

"I agree," Balloon said to him. Bart looked started for a few seconds, and then smiled.

"No bad jokes up there, huh?" he pointed upward.

"You'll see," Balloon said. A cup of Betty's good coffee besides her, Jane looked at the small gathering out of the entire town, all this part of Fork.

"This is it, Sam, yes. There are those who felt they were Christians but as they are soon to learn, they were only fooling themselves and they knew it all along. It will be the end of Wheatfield, and this part of Fork county there will be no more beasts, no more black masses, there will be nothing."

"Do you mean," Wayne asked, "this time we'll really beat the devil?"

"No." Balloon's reply was emphatic. "No mortal may ever beat the devil-only God. And only when he is ready. The Prince of Darkness will just be through here, that's all. And hopefully in a certain part of Canada, as well. And do not ask questions about that."

"When does God plan on beating the devil, Alex?" Wayne asked. Balloon said nothing.

"Strong silent type," kind of Bart said.

"Shut up," his wife told him. Bart sighed.

Chapter Six

"I don't know if I'll be able to lie to Roma," Sam said. "She'll see that I'm lying about what we saw and heard."

"Then…?"

"I don't know. I don't know what to do, how to start, or even where to start, really. This is all so mind bogging. Dad said the cross will protect us, but how much will the cross protect us? How about the way I feel about you? Will god," he stumbled over the word, "condone my lying? My feeling?"

"I don't know." She moved her gaze from Sam's face to the road ahead. Falcon house reared up. "We're about to find out," she said tensely.

"A joke?" Roma said. "What a very bad joke to play." She could not read his thoughts and that told her Sam was lying. It also told her that someone, probably Balloon, was interfering; that he had been in some sort of communication with his son. That was nothing new to her. People could and did move quite freely from the other side of the death line, providing one had the right connection with the Master of whatever world. She peered hard at Sam but she could not read his thoughts. She looked at her daughter and for the first time since Nadia's birth, her mother could not read her. And Nadia realized she had blocked her mother out.

"Don't look so upset, mother," she said innocently, the double meaning not lost on Roma. Roma's returning gaze was tight. She managed a small smile.

"A joke? Who would play such a joke on you? Bring you all the way to Montreal for a joke?"

"Kids back at Nelson, I suppose," Sam said.

"Well," Roma said, "it's over. You both returned and we have more guests. We'll have a gala time this week. Both the east and the west wings are alive with young people."

"And the devil," Sam thought. He looked hard at Roma, thinking, "Fuck you, and bitch!" She merely smiled. "Ugly," Sam fired his thoughts, "ugly and old, vain and stupid." The smile remained fixed, even softened just a bit. "And Still I'll bet you're a sorry screw!" Her expression did not change.

"You both must be tired from the hurried drive," Roma said. "Why don't you have a bit of a rest and get cleaned up, join your friends later?"

"They are not my friends," Nadia said. "A very few I get along with, the rest are creeps."

"They are our guests!" Her mother's tone was sharp. "And we will be civil to them."

"I will ignore them whenever possible." Nadia stood her ground for the first time in her life. High color rose to Roma's cheeks.

"We shall discuss this later."

"No need for that, mother." The reply was calmly stated. "I've said what I plan to do, and that is that." Roma was inwardly fuming but she managed a slight smile.

"Balloon has worked his crappy Christian magic on my daughter," she thought. "I wonder how many times over the years that sanctimonious stud has meddled in Nadia's affairs, and mine? No matter. For this time I have him boxed; he cannot be in two places at once, no matter if he is as obstinate as the warrior Michael, and just as Militant as you wish."

"Nadia," Roma said, "I must confess, you do have a great deal of your father in you at times."

"Yes," Nadia smiled, "and I cannot tell you how proud that makes me."

"I 'all break you." Roma stared hard at the young woman. She shifted her gaze to Sam. "And I'll break you as well. And when you are both mine, I'll breed you and have a grandchild that will make the Master proud. And if I May's do that, young people, then I'll give Nadia to Falcon to do with as he pleases, and I assure you, daughter, that will be an experience you will not savor."

"We'll see you at dinner," Sam said, taking Nadia's hand. The gesture did not go unnoticed by the mother.

"She is very angry," Nadia said.

"Not nearly as angry as she'll be when she sees that cross around your neck."

"Or the burn on your chest. Probably be best if we don't swim after this."

"That was to be my next suggestion." She squeezed his hand as they walked down the hall to their rooms.

"Sam? I'm not afraid any longer. I don't know whether that's good or bad."

"But neither am I. Wonder why?"

"I don't know."

"And I'll tell you something else. I cannot think of you as my sister."

"Then don't."

"How come," Sam said, his grin identical to his father's mischievous grin, "if I'm supposed to be so holy, all of a sudden my thoughts are so sexy?"

"I don't know about that." Her hips brushed his. the touch charged with such electricity, with wanton longing. "But mine aren't exactly pristine."

"Are we both awful?" Sam's question was spoken in all seriousness.

"No." The young woman's reply held the same weighty tone. "I think we're just being honest.

"What do we do about it?" They walked slowly through the great house.

"Give it some time," she said. They were at her door. She lifted her eyes to his.

"I'll keep the door among our bedroom locked."

"It's to be my decision alone?" She said," My mind is all ready made up." She opened the door and stepped into her room. The door closed softly behind her. Sam showered quickly and dried off, stepping into underwear shorts. He padded barefoot into his bedroom to stand in front of the floor-to-ceiling mirror. The dark thick mat of hair on his chest looked strange with the burned on scar of the cross directly in the center. He wondered if the hair would grow back. He gazed into the mirror reflection.

"I have a mission," he repeated his father's words, speaking in a whisper, "and it can destroy me. I will be tempted, and fall into temptation." He wondered if his father had been writing of Nadia or Roma, or both? Then he decided his father had been referring to Roma. He stepped away from the mirror and carefully hid the containers of holy water. He opened the manila envelope and sat on the edge of the bed studying the 8x10 of his father. He was still gazing at the 8x10 when the knock sounded on the door. Slipping into a robe, Sam opened the door. Adam Green stood in the hall just smiling at him. Sam opened, Adam stuck out his hand.

"Bet you're surprised to see me." It was spoken in a greasy manner. The two young men did not get along well. Although the same age, Adam was a senior while Sam, a junior. Adam was a sly, sneaky type, the kind Sam didn't like. Sam shook the offered hand. It was clammy and soft. Sam resisted the urge to wipe his hands on his robe.

"Yes, I am." Tom didn't tell us that he had invited you and the others. Adam grinned lewdly.

"Thought you'd have Nadia all to yourself, huh?" Sam stared at him just long enough for Adam to feel uncomfortable under unblinking gaze.

"I think he'll excuse… "

"Me?" Adam flushed hotly, clenching his hands into a fist at his side. "Well, there always one, I guess always one person that has to screw up a good thing."

"Meaning me, Adam?"

"You might learn a thing or two up here Sam. It should be interesting.

"Maybe more than you realize," Sam replied. Adam's smile was ugly. He walked away without shutting the door. Sam turned at a slight noise behind him, tensing then relaxing as the connecting door into Nadia's Room opened. She stepped into the room and Sam closed the hall door. Locking it. "I 'vet got an idea, Sam," she said, moving closer to him. He could smell The clean scent of the bath soap. And the ends of her black raven hair were slightly damp from the shower. A pulse beat strongly in her throat. "It was not a holy union," his father's words returned to him. Sam could see she was wearing nothing under her robe from the waist up. He could but guess about the waist down. If anything, it was blessed by the Dark One. Sam pushed his father's words from his mind.

"I'll be glad to hear your ideas, Nadia," his voice was husky. "I sure don't have any."

"Boy, what a lie! Your dad can not like this," she warned taking another step to him.

"My dad dumped this mission in my lap." Sam's tone was a bit sarcastic. "And if you're listening, dad, I 'm sorry but I don't know what to do"

"Let's play along for a time," she suggested. "I mean, may we leave?"

"I don't think so."

"I found out my mother May's read me as before and I suspect your dad had something to do with that. But the strangest thing has happened, Sam." He arched an eyebrow at her pause, very much aware that that was not the only part of him that was beginning to arch upwards. He resisted an impulse to fold his hands over his crotch. "I may pick up on your thoughts now," she said, smiling. "And yes, Sam, I am wearing panties."

"And she chose not to wear a bra," the thought popped into Sam's mind.

"You see?" she said. "It's not exactly reading a mind as much as guessing accurately what the other has done or is about to do."

"She wants me to kiss her." Sam sensed that mental push very strongly.

"So do it, Sam, before I change my mind." He stepped off the short distance among them with as much mixed emotion as when he first hurled himself out the open door of a plane back in jump school. The one main difference being he recalled he did not have a hard-on back then.

"How crude," Nadia whispered. She was slightly tense as his hands cupped.

"Face it; we're going to have to do something about this new power of ours."

"First things first," she said, her lips trembling as her hands found his lean waist and pulled him to her. Sam kissed her mouth, her throat, her neck, as their hips met in a frontal assault. As frenzied and attack as storming a beachhead, and then as they both would later recall, events began. Happening as if they were really above it all, watching two distinctly different begins in the room. Her gown dropped to the carpet in a silken rustle of fabric, and his eyes became as greedy as his searching mouth. She pulled the waist cord to his robe and it parted. One touch from her hand and a shrug of his shoulder and his robe made contact with the gown on the floor. Her panties were no more than a thin strip of almost diaphanous silk. The lushness of womanhood vividly outlined a perfumed jungle at the resting.

"At the completion of gently curving belly I am not perfection," she told him.

"Though mingling and meeting invisibly you are to me," he replied. She wore nothing except the gold cross, nestling among her breasts. His shorts joined her panties on the floor and they were content to stand naked in the center of the room, their lips touching gently, minds speaking volumes of silent words.

"I May's believe its wrong," she said.

"Nor I." She ran her hands down his flat ridged belly to grasp his maleness, fingers encircling the thickness. "Will it hurt me?" she asked, her voice throaty with passion, and trebly from anticipation, and he knew she was telling him she was a virgin,

"I don't know." The bed seemed the most logical place to answer any amount of questions, and they were soon there without either of them realizing they had traveled the short distance. "His lips found the hardness of nipple and his tongue brought them to jutting nubs of excitement while his hand traveled over the silkiness of belly to touch the edge of public hair and beyond, touching, lingering, fondling the wet lips and extended clitoris, finally moving to caress and part the folds of her-entering the soul of womanhood while she breathed words into his mouth. As they clung to each other, joined at the lips, she found his maleness, hard and anxious and with a knowledge that is inbred began stroking him, finding to her astonishment and delight the muscle of love thickening and hardening even more under her soft hand.

She clutched almost frantically at him whispering, "Now, Sam! Now!" he shifted on the bed and was among her legs positioning him. He gently placed the source of his manhood against the outer fold of woman and gently pushed, penetrating only a bit. She sighed under him arching her hips upwards, willingly asking for and receiving more of what she had desired since the moment of introduction only a few hours before. Sam slowly and with a tiny bit of pain pushed the length of him into the hot wetness of woman, then slowly withdrew, and from that moment on it was a battle with no loser-a war of silk and fire and passion; an ageless confrontation among man and woman. But it was more than that. It was a time of pain and pleasure for both of them as they dueled on the bed, turning the sheets into a satiny battleground, a mixture of scents. A tangle of flesh, it seemed to them to stop time, to halt the forward movement of that which is unstoppable, except for that brief time the cessation of the heart and soul, exciting the cooling flesh. Nadia began low whimpering sounds, shedding a few hot tears. Not from pain or guilt, although one of those would come later, but from the knowledge the signals to her body were sending to her brain, that this deliciousness this first time that would never again be the same, was about to end. Several small orgasms had shaken her, wavering almost sinfully through her, but as that one huge climax began to grip on her, she fought to hold on. But it was not to be. She grabbed almost too tightly at Sam's shoulders, pulling his mouth to hers, as a feeling unlike anything She had ever before experience ripped through her like the bow of ice cutter charging through thick ice. Sam exploded within her, his juices mingling with hers, a volcanic eruption of fluid that spreads its warmth around the silken walls of the ultimate entrapment of the male and female. Nadia wrapped her legs around his and pulled him to her until it seemed there was only one person on the bed. A huge, double headed, many limed creature. She shivered slightly as he softened within her, and she signed as he withdrew from this battle. Not retreating, merely recouping resources. She kissed him, and he returned the touching of lips with a gentleness that was almost sad. They slept together, and the two were not alone. Sam awakened once at the sound of a gentle knocking on the door. The hall was empty, but two trays of food were besides the door. He took the trays in and placed then on the dresser. He wasn't hungry and Nadia was deep in sleep. He crawled back into bed and she nestled her warmth against him. The food was forgotten.

Chapter Seven

"I have been blocked," Falcon said to Roma. "I cannot tell what is happening with Balloon son and Nadia. Is he interfering?"

"Indirectly, I believe. Through Balloon I am sure my daughter and Sam now have powers even they do not realize they possess, and I do not understand that."

"I have attempted to speak with the Master but I have been unable to and that distresses me, Roma." Falcon lingered over the word, drawing it out as his mind raced.

"Perhaps, yes! I sense the battleground had been marked; the Master of light and the Prince of Darkness have finally agreed on something."

"They haven't agreed on anything for thousands of years except their mutual dislike of each other." She was silent as the implication of his words struck home.

"You mean… you believe we are alone in this? That neither Master will interfere any further?"

"For now, yes, I do."

"For how long?"

He shrugged eloquently, and then put a finger to Roma's lips, a gesture of caution. "But I believe this, darling, should we fail here we are through on earth." She thought about that for a moment-her marred by ugliness, of her deliberations. She laughed nastily. Things seemed to be repeating themselves.

"I 'm beginning to believe our Master's sense of humor is equaled only by the lack of trust, worthiness, and loyalty."

"I hope you know what you are saying, for I surely don't."

"My sins, I hate that word, my sins have come home to roost."

She smiled. "Isn't that a quaint expression?"

"A colloquialism, really. I picked it up in Georgia right after the civil war among the states I plotted against. Someone in this house is plotting against me."

"It is not I."

Falcon drew himself to his full height, indignant that she would even think him quality of such treason.

She laughed darkly. "No," she said, patting his arm, "not you, Falcon. Even for a warlock you have an inordinate sense of honor and loyalty and we have known and liked each other for too many centuries.

"Then that leaves only…" He refused to speak the name, but Roma had no such reluctance.

"Yes, my son, Tom. He is strange even for us and he is also young, ambitious, and I have to confess it, he possesses my genes, and none of his father's genes are in him. But surly the young man realizes his power is not yet equal to yours, and will not be until he leaves this life and assumes his true role in the ways of the arts." Falcon shook his head.

"But you are right. Tom is odd, even for us." Her gaze silenced him.

"I don't wish to discuss my son's pederasty tendencies."

"It is not forbidden by our Master."

She signed and waved her hand. "But you are correct, of course he does go too far at times, but I have had many offspring. Some good, some bad!" A thought sprang into her mind; a thought she did not share with Falcon.

"If we are alone here," Falcon mused, "I wonder if the same applies in Wheatfield."

"Probably. I feel Balloon is there looking after his precious Jane. I never could understand what he saw in her. No tits."

"Explain a golem to me, Alex." Jane said. They were in her home after having spent hours with Bart and Betty, Wayne and Anita. Tony and some of his friends from the coven had been to the house, and had in the house, and the vernacular of young, trashed it, writing filthy sentences on the walls, stating plainly what they were going to do with Jane. But Balloon's bible had not been touched. It sat on the small table like a sentry or duty. Jane had Cleaned up the house and painted over the nasty words and obscene drawings.

"There is no such thing as a golem." Balloon thrust his reply. "But that. Creature standing in the corner in Wayne's living room! Yes."

"Then it is real?"

"All things are real. Evil is real."

"Alex, you're being vague."

"In a sense, but really I am telling you all that I may."

"All right," she said after a time, "I think I'll see if we believe in it."

"It is real. But if someone does not believe, it doesn't exist."

She waved her hand toward the outside. "But will they believe in it?"

"Oh, yes, is assured of that. God must have a sense of humor-he created humans didn't he?" And the clock in the hall chimed its message-it was Thursday.

Horror was about to begin!

Sam awakened with his arms full of soft, warm nakedness, and his heart pounding, but he did not awaken with a start. He wondered why his heart was hammering so violently in his chest. He opened his eyes, looking around the dimly lit room on the dresser, and remembered bringing them in. Nothing else was disturbed. He glanced at his watch on the nightstand and knew then what had awakened him. It was just past midnight. Thursday-but what's so special about Thursday? The day of Satan's worship, of course. He gently brought Nadia out of her sleep.

"I love you," she whispered, "and I don't think it is wrong." She smiled. "I must look so awful."

"No, you're beautiful." He picked up his watch. "Look at the time."

"Oh, God! No wonder no one checked on us."

"What do you mean?"

"It's Thursday night: They all are at the circle of stones behind the house. I used to ask them what they did out there, but I would get no answer. I finally Quit asking-something about star-gazing was what they finally settled on. I never did believe it."

"Nadia? You're holding something back from me."

"Yes."

"Tell me"

"It… isn't time, Sam. I will, I promise." He thought of her statement in the four-wheeler about knowing allot about him. He shrugged it off.

"You mentioned something about that circle of stone this afternoon while we were eating at the park. It triggered something in me then, and the same thing happened now. There's something about that circle that is whispered about back in Wheatfield. Used to be, anyway." He paused, "Sure, now I remember. Kids used to say that was where the Devil lived. That must be where dad met the Devil. Oh, damn, Nadia! How much is not? What in God's name are we supposed to do?"

“I don’t know.”

“I do know this: I want to see this circle of stone. We’ll go out there tomorrow.”

”Are you out of your mind?” He ignored that, for he believed he just might be, for a amount of reasons.

”May we see it from the house?”

“Faintly, from that window,” she pointed, “But you May’s see it at night.” He slipped from her warmth and blew out the small lamp, plunging the room into darkness he opened the drapes.

“Nadia!” he called, “we may see it.”

”What do you mean?” She crawled from the big bed and came to stand besides him. She gasped at the sight. In the small clearing behind the house it was torch-lit. “I‘ve never seen that before,” she said.

“It’s begun,” Sam said flatly, without fear, and Nadia picked up on the firmness in his voice. The ten days have begun.

“Sam, what ten days have begun? What are you talking about? What ten days?” He looked at her in the darkness of the room.

”Ten days, honey. We have... they have ten days. Don’t ask me how I know and I‘ll tell you something else-my knowing scares the hell out of me!”

Chapter Eight

In Wheatfield, around the circle of stones, as was behind Falcon House, the pledge was being chanted, "I renounce God the Father, the Son, and God the Holy Spirit," and in both places the beasts growled their approval. "I renounce and deny my Creator, the Holy Virgins, the Saints, Baptism, Father, Mother, Relation, Heavens, Earth, and all this world contains that is Good, Pure and Sacred." They lifted their arms straight out in front of them and screamed, "Praise the Power of the Prince of Darkness for only he is the true Master to all that's Evil. I give my body and mind to Satan. Praise is his name, my Master. None other than him, this I swear by all that is Unholy." And the Beasts of Satan howled their agreement, their eyes and wild jaws, leaking drool. The beasts began dancing an obscene hunching and howling dancing to the beat of the music they alone could hear.

"Is there a gun in this house?" Sam asked as they dressed. The drapes were closed, the room lighted somehow. They both felt much more comfortable with the lights on.

"Yes, Falcon enjoys shooting." She grimaced a sudden distaste.

"What's wrong?"

"He likes to see animals suffer. He's an expert shot, but I've overheard the servants talking down through the years that he'll deliberately shoot an animal where it will take the longest to die. He lives to listen to a wounded animal scream."

"Nice fellow." Sam muttered. "The servants? You mean may we trust them?"

"No, I don't think so. They have all been with Roma for as long as I may remember, especially David Johnson. That's not the right word he's a zombie."

"You can be more right than you think about that," Sam told her. "Come on, let's see this gun room. I want to see what Falcon has in stock." They walked down the dimly lit hall, walking quietly but not stealthily in case they met someone unexpected and aroused suspicion. Nadia stopped him at a doorway.

"The first of the guest rooms in this wing," she whispered. "This would be Tom's room. All the boys' rooms are on the right and the girls' are on the left."

"You take the girls rooms and I'll take the boys," he told Nadia. Only Jim and Jeff were in their beds. When Sam tried to wake them, he could not. They were sleeping as if they were drugged, which he concluded, they probably were. Across the hall, five were in their beds: Judy, Mary, Carol, and Linda. Gently then roughly, she could not wake them. He did the same to the other. It seemed as if they were sleeping the sleep of the dead. And then Sam took notice of the gold medallion on a chain around their necks.

"They all have been drugged," he told Nadia.

"I guess from now on we'd better watch what we eat and drink. I'll bet you those trays of food that was left outside of our room was drugged also. That's why no one checked on us. Mother always uses the buffet line when we have this many guests-at least that's been her routine in the past."

"Routine may be very dangerous," Sam said, remembering his training. "Lull one into a false sense of security." Nadia smiled. His sergeant Sam slipped his hand around her waist and let his hand slip down to the curve of her buttocks. He gently caressed her.

"Don't start something you May's finish," she said, "And here in the hall would be a perfectly dreadful place to be caught making love." Sam removed his hand. She stopped them before they entered the foyer. They had to cross to get to the gun room on the second floor.

"I just remembered something. Falcon has a reject room in the basement. He spends hundreds of dollars, maybe thousands on guns every year. If there is the slightest flaw, scratch on the stock, a tiny bit of bluing that's wrong, anything.... he won't have it. He just throws it in the reject room and forgets it."

"He doesn't return them?"

"No, never."

"That's the place for us, then. Take one of his favorite guns, he'd probably miss it. Where are the servants' quarters?"

"That way," she said, pointing. "First floor, in the back."

"Come on. I want to check there, too." The servants' quarters were all empty. "That answers another question," Sam said. "Come on, we'd better hurry." He wondered how long the ceremony at the circle of stone would last.

"It breaks up before dawn," she said with a grin. "It can really come in handy before all this is over."

"I wonder how far we may project and read each others thoughts."

"We'll try tomorrow." She tugged at his arm, "Today, I mean."

"Come on; let's get to the reject room." Sam selected a good shotgun and a high-powered rifle, and then picked a pistol for Nadia. The weapons were all in good condition except for they needed cleaning and oiling. They were fine weapons from skilled manufactures. He stuffed his pockets with cartridges and Nadia did the same. She was nervous, wanting to leave, but Sam wanted to prowl. He found a tarp-covered cache of camping equipment, and loaded them both down with shelter halves, blankets, rope, and tent pegs. They filled two packs, and then filled two smaller knapsacks. Finally, Sam picked up two pairs of binoculars and steered Nadia toward the door.

"I feel like a beast of burden," she complained on the way back to their rooms. "Why do we need all these coils of rope, Sam?" Sam stopped in the dimly lit hall. "What's wrong, Sam?"

"Beast, why did that word spark something in me?"

"Tom hasn't been trying to frighten you, has he?"

"What do you mean?"

"He likes to tell people about monsters that roam the timber in the back of the house. No, he wouldn't tell you, he likes to tell girls to frighten them. No, it's more than that. Has something to do with Wheatfield, rumors of Beasts of The Devil creatures."

"Are there beasts in the timber?"

"I… don't know Sam. I've seen something, heard noises and sounds that were not human, could not be human, but yet really not an animal either. But more animal than human, if that makes any sense to you. And once, when I was about, oh, maybe ten years old, I went behind the back of our house and came across the circle of stone, mother told me never go there. The smell that came out of the hole in the ground was hideous. When I walked closer, I don't know how to explain this, the growl that came out of that hole was not menacing as much as if whatever it was in there was telling me to stay away. These sounds

Chapter Nine

But how I warn you? We don't Sam flung the thought into her brain she has to find out the true course herself. How do you know that? She silently asked calmly eating her breakfast. I just do someone... or something is telling me perhaps later they will tell me differently. And Sam counted Susan" as amid the lost when she said: Tom is taking me on a hike this afternoon says he wants to show me some ancient stones. He gave me this she pulled at the gold medallion Sam had noticed her wearing when he saw her sleeping. Mr. Falcon offered one just like it to Lana and Linda and Judy. The medallion of the damned of the Devil. Stupid, Lana refused hers, Susan said so did Linda, and Judy, I just cannot believe you did that how rude it's just too expensive a gift, Susan I just don't think it's right to take something that expensive." Susan's eyes glittered as dangerously as a snake before striking. The venomous look faded and she returned to her breakfast eating in silence for a moment, then she abruptly left the table without Lana's going to be all right Nadia fired the thought.

"I don't know," Sam disagreed, "I don't think so. She's playing some sort of game."

"I think I just lost a friend." Lana said glumly, she was a small, very petite red head girl, with deficit features deep brown eyes and a lush little figure.

"Then she wasn't much of a friend to begin with." Sam told her.

"I really don't, well don't take this the wrong way, Nadia," Lana said, "and I don't believe you will, but I am kind of sorry I came up here." she's lying! Sam projected. Nadia ignored the thought I know, "Lana I don't like most of my brother's friends, neither does Sam." She started to warn the girl about her mother, the house, but the words would not form on her lips she struggled to speak

"She shut her mouth you see?" Sam scolded her, "you May's know for a fact that she is lying, I know only the words that comes into my head but I thought your God? Nadia, was just God," Nadia flung the challenging Question.

"He is, but he also helps those who help themselves and cannot tolerate a liar."

"I don't understand but I will accept what you say that's half the battle honey." Sam then remembered something the recollection coming so strongly it hit his mental process with the impact of a tidal wave. His bible! He had never unpacked it from his arrival at Nelson Jonestown College and it was still there in the bag in his room… at Falcon house an unexpected ally we have an excellent library here, Nadia was telling Lana all the latest novels I 'all show you where it is and maybe you may find something you'd like read, Oh, I 'd love that could I maybe dine with you two all the time if it's okay?" Sure Sam said that way maybe I may figure out what you're scheming sure you may eat with us she squeezed his hand thanks, Sam you're the nicest guy I know she was gone from the table before Sam could reply. Umm!" Nadia said, humor creeping into her eyes I have some competition.' "Nah." Sam brushed it off him leaned close and whispered: besides I like girls with big tits.'

The silence that hung over Wheatfield was heavy and evil like a hot humid day, it clung to people enveloping them in a stinking shroud those who thought they had fooled the almightily as easily as they could not understand they prayed to God, but they lied in their hearts too many times and even now, their prayers were insincere they watched as the phone company personnel pulled the plugs to their phones, cutting them off from the outside world. They sensed evil and danger all around them and tried to flee in their cars and trucks. But they could not get out of town. They returned to their homes and waited in fear for the unknown to occur. They called their pastors, but the church pulpits had long ago been filled with those who worship another God and the preachers laughed at them, some of them making evil deals, will the husbands save you? The preachers questioned. All Right your life, for your wife.' It's a deal, many husband cried pushing their wives into the arms of the ungodly. The wives Were taken and raped amid other acts committed against them. But the husbands found that to bargain with the Devil is a fool's game and they would learn that very painfully in the Lance house the golem stirred as invisible life was breathed into it. John watched it slowly shuffle across the floor, it ponderous legs and massive arms moving like some primal creature just awakened from a million years of ice locked sleep, it bumped its head on the archway and stopped, looking almost stupidly around the room, the slits that were item eyes having no expression. Wayne came into the room and took the huge clay man's hand as one might a child. Is it time?" he asked.

The golem nodded, gaining balance and understanding with each second.

"What did I call you? You got to have a name." The golem shrugged its solid shoulders. "I think I 'all call you Barney," the golem lifted its hands in a gesture of acquiescence as Betty and Anita huddled together against a far wall. Wayne sat with a faint smile on his lips. "That thing really understands what you're saying."

" I suppose so, Bart said it does." Betty walked from the corner of the room to look up at the huge clay man. "Well you May's walk around with no clothes on, it just isn't decent." The golem gazed down at the woman. "So I made you some pants to put on you, wait right where you are" she left the room, returning with a large pair of trousers, "denim," she said holding out the jeans for the golem. Difficult material to sew but I did it. The golem looked at Wayne, and Bart said "momma the golem don't know about pants, what's he got to have pants for?"

"Because I said he's got to that's why. If he's going to be our care taker he's got to look nice." At least the four of them managed to get the jeans on the golem and surprisingly, Wayne patted the golem on the arm. Joey Lewis, you aunt Barney, but you got class. The golem lumbered out of the room, bumping his head as he went out of the door. He sat downs atone the porch, waiting. Wayne picked up his shotgun, checking the loads. Bart did the same. The four of them Sat in the living room waiting. Waiting for the evil to begin, waiting for the horror they knew was coming, waiting the night, waiting and praying they had enough faith to get them through it.

"Did you have anything to do with my friend's decision to remain in Wheatfield? Jane asked.

"Wayne made his decision when he shut down the newspaper, Bart when he sold his store. Tony, He lost his faith years ago, young Sam was only a child. Tony is evil. The world is a pretty crappy place isn't it Alex?"

"Father Decoys and I discuss that same topic from time to time you make it sound like old home week the misty face smiled. Heavens is not what most mortals envisions, I may assure you of that. But, I may tell you no more I wish this were over yes.' I want to go home.' You will is it lovely ....there?

"It is Peaceful? Quiet? Am I going to suffer before I go?"

"I **cannot lie yes."**

"Bart and Doris? Wayne and Anita?"

"Anita is not very strong, they will suffer to a degree, but mine will be physical. It was not spoken as a question. Balloon said nothing. "Your silence tells me I 'm right.." Jane sighed "I will endure it '. yes," the thought pushed into her brain.

"And so must I, they're leaving" Roma said to Falcon heading into the woods, she swore a venomous string of curses.

"It is difficult for me to believe I have birthed a Christian. It's disgusting! Where did we fail, Falcon?" he laugh at her.

"We didn't, Roma, put such thoughts out of your head." Balloon interfered that's all. 'His seed must have been strong like a hot river.' You still remember?"

"I shall never forget it. I mounted him a half a dozens times before he lost The battle and I couldn't keep him inside me. Tell me Roma did you cheat?" she seemed astonished he would even ask such a foolish question.

"Of course! That is the answer to your question, and many more unmasked questions why Tom is deceitful and plotting for one. Balloon's seeds were many pure and strong with most of them forming Nadia, Tom is weak and he is scheming weak in many other areas: I've know that for many other areas: I've know that for many years we must not lean too heavily on him you know of course, he cheated taking his difficult military she whirled about, her face flushed he swore to me he would not but he did I wanted to tell you wanted to see how that deception affected him I will tell you this and you know I am a warrior, Tom will be no match for your young Sam I sensed something else as well, Roma the young man has killed and not just in the heat of open battle I sense he has killed, once at least probably several times , on orders from his government covertly and cold-bloodedly?"

"When you were able to see his thoughts study his innermost character, how had the killing affected him?"

Falcon paused lighting his pipe sending billowing clouds of fragrant smoke swirling about him, the silence only heightened the moment, "not at all," he finally said. "The young man is a true warrior, and you know how he; Falcon cast his eyes upward feels about warriors. Young Sam is his father's son." Roma smiled entirely. Her smile grew wicked. Falcon read her thoughts.

"Roma...?" she met his eyes, dark evil gazing into dark evil,

"Yes, Falcon?"

"It's too dangerous; you're much too old for that nonsense. Birthing the twins almost killed you or have you forgotten?"

"No, but, I failed with them and now if your deductions are correct and I believe they are I know why, it would not be that way with young Sam, you would not cheat?"

"You my dear," he chuckled. "Anyway, Roma it's out of the question For a amount of reasons, paramount amid them the fact young Sam is in love with his half sister, and she with him. They're practically nauseating with it. Besides, I forbid you to take the chance." He turned his head, smiling as he spoke. He was not disappointed with her reaction. She gave him a look that would have stopped a runaway truck dead in the road.

"You Forbid it." She screamed at him "forbid! You do not forbid me to do a fucking thing!"

Falcon signed. "And I worked so hard improving your vocabulary, taking it from the gutter now you revert.

"Forbid me! Are you forgetting who is in charge here?"

"Not at all my dear, calm you. I was merely attempting to be practical about this matter. Roma consider the risk factor, one.. Even if you should seduce the young man without cheating, having a demon child would kill you. That is written, secondly: the master would surely void your plan. Oh, Roma go fuck the young man, anyway you may, and get it out of your system then forget it, we have matters of much greater urgency here." She whirled and stalked from the room cursing under her breath. Falcon watched her leave slamming the door. He stood and slowly shook his head a pity he thought to be so obsessed by the memory or Balloon she fell in love itch a man of God. He shuddered at the thought of how degrading they stopped watching us; Nadia said I could feel her eyes when they left me.

"They're planning something . Evil. I just wish I knew what we are supposed to do about it."

"Do I have a free hand?"

"I don't know Nadia" we're stumbling around in the dark with this thing. I don't know what to do.

"Yes, all right, my dad appeared and wrote me a letter. I've convinced Myself we didn't dream it, a sign of the cross is burned, burned into my chest. Okay I 'all accept that I 'vet been chosen to do what? I have to assume that I am to follow in my dad's footsteps; do what he did back in Wheatfield in the fifties.". He stopped at the edge of the deep timber and sat on a rock, Nadia, besides him. "Dad was trying to tell us something about our being related but what? He said it wasn't a holy union. Does that make our feelings all right? I 'm going to say it does, I May's help the way I feel about you. We were drawn together from the first moment that we met, you felt it, and I felt it and we'll just leave it at that. Mother always said I was just like my dad. I guess the service proved it: It.... Really doesn't bother me to kill. I May's say much about it, although I don't know what it would matter now to you. I mean but sometimes special troops have to kill cold-bloodedly. A very few get picked to do that. I got picked. I did that several times no guilt feelings none at all. No remorse no nothing. I think Dad must have been like that. Okay, then I 'all do whatever in the hell, I 'm supposed to do. I'm hearing voices in my head; words pop out of my mouth that are alien to me; I know things that mortals aren't supposed to know and don't ask me to explain any of it. I May's so I 'all just have to wait until someone, or something gives me the green light with instruction." She put her arms around him and held him , gentleness, her understanding and that women are the more mercenary of the species "We'll both know when it's time Sam," she told him, holding him, "I believe that and I believe that our feelings for each other are right. And you must believe it." Holding hands, they walked into the timber and the silence of God's free nature seemed to make them stronger, and draw them closer to God. The mood was almost religious; the towering trees a non-de-nominal cathedral silently growing around the young couple. They came to a small rushing creek and sat on a rock by the bubbling waters. "Tell me more about being a Christians Sam."

"I don't know that much about it, Nadia I sometimes think it's a feeling one must have and I don't have it very often."

"I think you're a better person than you think."

"I've killed in cold-blood," he said softly.

'Yet you've been chosen by higher power to do something good here on earth." He looked at her.

"Killing your mother and brother probably. Have you thought about that Nadia?"

"Yes. But I have no feelings of love or affection for either of them Sam. I don't recall the last time I felt anything for them. I've always felt like a stranger around them, out of place unwanted and really unloved. I don't believe they know love, I'll put it stronger than that they worship Satan, so how may they know love?" His smile was gentle, full of admiration for her and love. "Do you believe in baptizing or sprinkling, Sam? I was baptized when I was just a kid. Too young really. You don't understand what it's all about at twelve or thirteen years old. It's exciting."

"Yeah, I guess either one would do I 'm not even sure it's necessary. How about the thief on the cross?" I know that story; I want to be a Christian. How may I baptize you? Do you remember the words Sam?"

"No I really don't. He searched his memory well. "I remember what Jesus said to the eleven disciples after the rock had rolled away or something like that."

"Oh Sam!" She laughed. "All right, that will have to do," say them. Does it do it? You mean here?

"Nadia I don't have the uh, authority."

"What authority does it take?"

"Well, I don't know exactly do you know you have it? I mean you're a baptized Christian aren't you? May's Christians baptize somebody?"

"I guess so, Nadia. But I 'm not about to stick you in that water." He said pointing to the creek, "you'd freeze to death!"

"Then put your fingers in the creek and do that other thing," he grinned at her, suddenly fading when he saw she was serious. Feeling very much like a fool, Sam kneeled by the fast rushing creek and wet his fingers he touched his finger—onto her forehead and said s, "Nadia, and I really hope someone is listening who knows what this is all about all' power is given unto me in Heaven, and on earth. Go ye therefore and teach all nations, baptizing them in the name of the Father, and of the Son, and of the Holy Ghost. Teaching them to observe all things whatsoever I have commanded you and to believe I am with you always, even unto the end of the world. And Sam Knew something all powerful had been guiding his voice, for he had not read that passage since he was a child.

Chapter Ten

He kissed her lips and said "I feel kind of like an idiot, Nadia."

"I really hope Jesus didn't add that," she said dryly.

"What do they represent?" Susan asked her eyes on the circle of stone. Tom moved closer to her, standing just behind the young woman she could smell the musk of his cologne and it was rich and heady, arousing some hereto force hidden urge deep within her. Tom breathed in deeply her perfume and places his hands on her shoulders. It is said that here is where ancient ceremonies were held, he told her. He now stood with his groin pushing against her buttocks, knowing she could feel his slight erection. He pushed against her; she made no effort to move away, "what kind of ceremonies?" She asked her voice low.

"The people, who worship here, Susan, worship a Master who allows them supreme pleasure in life. Their Master knows that mortals are susceptible beings and to place too many restrictions upon them is not wise. Are you a Christian, Susan?'

"I was baptized as a child, but I don't attend church,"

"Why not?" the talk at school is you're untouchable that Susan is super-cool all ice you're touching me so the talk must be wrong. They say you don't drink … anything.

"Like I said, Tom: The talk is all wrong." Susan pushed her buttocks against his heating swelling groin. He moved his hands from the shoulders to her slim waist, she said, "Tell me more about this religion, Tom. It sounds very intriguing.

"What would you like to know about it?" His hands were gently caressing her denim clad hips.

"Oh… like what is your church called? And I assume you believe belong to it yes many names depending on your local. Have I ever been to one of your churches?"

"I doubt it." He buried his face in the lushness of her hair and breathed the Scent of her.

"Why all this sudden attention to me, Tom? I've seen your looking at me Tom, at dances and school functions why have you never asked me out?"

"I didn't believe you would ever go out with me."

"Why?"

"Because of the talk."

"But I'm here, and we're alone.'" She turned in his arms and kissed him, running her tongue over his lips, pushing against him, working her hips against his, "did you bring blankets so we could fuck, Tom?" He laughed his lips still on hers I have to confess "I did, Susan,"

"all right" she said softly, then added "Lana and the others are so stupid they don't realize what happened, Tom but my father was a doctor the research kind I know when I 'vet been drugged beside I 'm a light sleeper; not like I slept last night you didn't have to do that Tom. He said nothing, she pulled away, opening her jacket then removing it. Tom gazed hungrily at the swell of her breasts pushing against her shirt she lifted the heavy gold medallion seems to be a great many of those Tom but I gave only one to you." Her eyes were serious as they gazed into the darkness of his eyes his were unreadable.

"I studied this medallion quiet closely this morning under a magnifying glass."

"And?"

"It was unusual I found myself captivated by the detail but not offended? Oh no. Some people are offended by the scene" and she sealed her fate when she said "I found myself wishing I was a participant did you now?"

"Yes you could be. Tell me what I would gain. If you're one of the lucky ones accepted by him everlasting beauty and life and fame I 'm a virgin, Tom I really am' why? Are you saving yourself, for the right man?" something like that. But I think me 'vet found him."Ved no, I guess not. My brother is amply Endowed, like you, she said glancing at him; my father must have been hung like a bull." She laughed what a marvelously elegant expression." Shall we hike through the timber and see what's happening?" Sam suggested with grin. What is another side of you? The voyeur?" I just want to see if dads gave him the same equipment."

"You're awful; you and Tom are about the same in that department."

"How would you know?"

"I'm his sister remember? I 'vet seen my brother naked on numerous occasions. None recently thank God," she was gently leading him in the opposite direction of the wailing pleasure sounds.

"Must be getting' good," Sam drawled "you're incorrigible!" Remember, Sam. , he has the same applies to you, she looked horrified. I forgot about that they walked a full mile from the circle of stone, before they spread the ground sheet Sam carried. He said we'll give them time to get done then wonder down that way. I want to see this circle of stones and the hole in the ground. She lay back on the ground sheet, her hands behind her head. Sam's eyes began wandering "don't get any ideas" she cautioned him, pointing upward. "He's watching"

A half continent away many of the residents of Wheatfield began answering the call of their chosen master, gathering in the huge clearing on the Saone Ranch, whose eastern range boarded on the fenced-in area known as the Digging. While God did not interfere directly into the affairs on earth, at least not too often, and certainly never in any obvious manner, Satan was bound by no rules on earth, and could do anything the dark one chose to do and did often, there would be no interference from any one in this part of Fork County. The Devil had seen to that. Should any one travel through, all would appear normal and no one would have any desire whatsoever to stop for anything, but the dark one did not know that God, also had plans for this part of Wheatfield, and was all ready working this time if all went according to Satan's Plans and the Prince of Darkness saw no reason why they should not. There would be no great billowing plums of smoke from burning, exploding buildings; no racing about the county blowing up farm houses and shooting people, none of that business, this time no all would be handled a bit more sedately this time . All around. His followers could, of course have a bit of fun; dance, sing, engage in their heretofore. Forbidden open orgies, all that kind of mortal frivolity. Perhaps some human offering would be fun certainly the Jew and that idiot aging reporter and his simpering wife would die and ten the master of grotesqueness would have his fun with Balloon's bitch. That would be worth the waiting; he pondered his option whether to pass her around amid the men until she died from exhaustion, or let the women have her, perhaps have a pony mount her. That would certainly be an interesting sight; there were not so many things to do with the Balloon's bitch. Well, he had time to think things through but behind all his smugness all his confidence that, at last he would finally beat that ageless cosmic meddler in the firmament was the thought of that maverick resident of that miserable place. Balloon, "why did he allow Balloon such liberties?" That puzzled Beelzebub. Balloon was not like many of course, there had been many others before Balloon. Hundreds down through the years but with few exceptions they had been such wimps, such a praying bunch of hand-wringing, psalms singing sister. And one fine warrior: It just wouldn't do to have many like him wandering about perhaps, Satan thought yes! Yes, there was a way. Maybe Balloon would take it. Not a chance, the words ripped into Satan's thoughts you have all ready extended yourself too much here on earth, Star-Wart," Satan replies: Don't press your luck." You cannot tempt Balloon." How do you know?" I know Balloon Bah I think perhaps you have a grown a bit too cocky of late you forget, I know your limitation here on earth. I know exactly what you may be able to do me .... If You mention I one more time, scratch I will certainly interfere with your plans. Directly." You wouldn't dare!"

"Try me." lasher of words

From the only thing in the universe he feared. "You will leave us alone here in Wheatfield?"

"I don't bargain with you."

"Not good enough."

"I will never bargain with you, Belial, you should know that by now."

"Afraid I might beat you, eh?"

The heavens were silent.

"Oh, all right!" the tempter pouted but you have to give me something to seal the bargain,"

"I told you Hooded-One: I do not bargain with.

"What is so special about Balloon? You may tell me that, at least."

"The heavens were silent Ah! Of course!" the Mephistophelian, voice cracked, "I see. Baby yes. You rather like him don't you? You don't have to reply I know. Yes while you're pet. Michael is out flitting about the about the heavens, you'd like Balloon sitting with you, eh? You do like your pet dogs Balloon don't you, Is Michael there now?"

The Heavens rumbled as the archangel voiced his objection to being called a dog. Satan laughed, and lightning licked across the sky, "turn your militant loose, thunder; let him face me let me see if his powers are as great as mine." That was the wrong thing for the Dark one to suggest.

The heavens were calm, even while Satan howled and cursed and called down malisons on all the residents of the firmament. He received no reply.

Chapter Eleven

That enraged the ruler of filth. Satan fired his thoughts into the head of Jean Johnson. "You have sampled nearly all of the men around you Bitch!" he said, still smarting from his conservation with the Holy One. "Pick five of the most virile men that you have, and have them ready to receive Balloon's precious whore."

And on the Johnson Ranch on the plains the dancing began, preparatory to the Friday night sacrifice. The coven members danced lewdly, hunching obscenely as they shouted filth to the heavens. They was not afraid in their vocal and physical defilements for the Prince of Evil had assured them his protection: guaranteed them a long and lustful life on earth. These coven members these worshipers of darkness, these students of bell-book-and candle they had made any amount of mistaken in their evil lives. But paramount amid them believed anything the Devil said, while forgetting that one true God is a vengeful God.

"Let's see how far out thoughts will carry,' "Sam suggested. "We'd better know, because I think things are going to get down to the nut-cutting pretty quick"

"I do love your expression Sam," Nadia said smiling. Baring in mind he was a Minster, probably so mother often said he was real character would speak his mind whenever and yet he has God's favor. I don't understand that.

"From what little I know of God's word I always thought of Christians as rather meek and mild types."

"Oh, I think that's a dangerous misconception, Nadia, God loves his warriors. I think Michael sits at God's side some even think he is God's bodyguard. Others think of him as the hand of retribution," she glanced at him, thinking: "yes, I believe God does love his warriors." They separated in the timber, walking first a few hundreds apart testing their capacity to project and receive thoughts; they found that distance did make a difference in the receiving and sending.

"Let's this circle of stone," Sam said

"What if we run into Tom and Susan?"

He grinned at her thinking, how beautiful she was in the light filtering through the timber, "we'll just ask them how it was."

She playfully pushed him away. "Sam, you're impossible!" The circle of stone was deserted when they got there. They looked for Tom and Susan, finding only the still-pressed down blanket of pine needles where they had lain. Sam kneeled down, studying with great interest the largest stone, which depicted scenes of great depravity: of men with huge hutting phalluses of women with their legs spread wide exposing the genitalia: scenes of mass orgies men with small children: scenes of hideous torture of grotesque creating, monsters, leaping and snarling. And finally on the east side of the boulder a scene depicting a saintly looking man who was locked in some sort of combat with a beastly appearing creature. Sam looked up from his studying,

"You didn't tell me about this." Her face was pale.

"That was never there before, Sam. I mean, the rocks, yes, but not all those carvings," Nadia he let his statement drift away here," you just couldn't see them. They are probably exposed only when Satan wants them to be."

"And, how do you know all that?" he silently questioned his mind, or when he is near she said tightly. "Yes." Sam rose from his squat position, and put his arms around her she was trembling "I 'm scared Sam, for the first time I 'm really frightened. Now I know what you meant when you said you didn't know what to do where to start. Sam comforted her as best he could, for he too was frightened.

"Come on. Let's see this hole in the ground.' They smelled the stench long before they came to the hole both their noses wrinkling at the foul odor, "may you imagine that his father had said almost the same thing to a couple of his friends back in, 56' standing near the Digging. Gross!" Nadia said

She watched as Sam reached into his jacket pocket. His face paled. He jerked his hand from the pocket as if he had touched a snake.

"What's wrong Sam?" His face regained a bit of color after his initial shock, "that ....that's not my pistol in there."

"What!"

"I thought just a moment ago, when I was kneeling down by that boulder there was too much weight in my pocket. But I shrugged it off.

"that's not a .38 revolver. That's a.... Automatic, let's see,"

Sam looked at her for a moment and then put his hand into his jacket, he said. "Oh, my God !"

"Sam!" He pulled out his hand, the hand containing three fully loaded clips for a 45. Automatic pistol. What kind of gun did your father carry back in Wheatfield?"

"I don't know."

"Take out the pistol, Sam."

The young man hesitantly put his hand back into his pocket, gingerly pulling out the big automatic. He checked it. A full clip in the butt he turned the weapon and saw a brass nameplate embedded and riveted into the handle. SGT. Alex Milton Balloon, Japan 1956. "It's ....it belonged to my father," he choked out the words, holding the weapon out for Nadia to see the brass plate in the grip. She put a hand to her mouth and face and turned pale with shock,

"Something else just popped into my head, Sam said. "John Thomas told me one time my father sure could use a Thompson submachine gun. My mother gave him a look that would have fried eggs what's a Thompson submachine gun?"

"An old kind of Tommy gun like the gangsters use to use."

"Are they any good?" Sam smiled up about a hundred yards; "if a Thompson won't stop what's coming at you, with those big old slugs Honey, then it won't be stopped."

"I would love to have just one?"

"No," but it wouldn't take me long to learn." He looked at the pistol again, somehow and he could not shake the feeling the weapon felt natural in his hands, almost as if he had held before.

"What are you thinking, Sam? Although she knew his thoughts he told her maybe that's what your father wants you to feel?

"Yeah" he said softly a sudden sensation of being pulled into a dark force field enveloped them.

"Sam!" Nadia cried, taking his hand.

"What's happening?"

"Hang on. I don't know." They sank to the ground and they were speechless, immobile as the strange force took control. Time took them mentally winging into darkness, spinning them wildly through multicolor.

They watched a naked man fighting with a naked woman. The faces were blurred, but both Sam and Nadia knew who they were: Alex Balloon and Roma. Articles of clothing and pieces of equipment flew about the struggling couple sailing in a slow circle. The man struck the woman with his fist and her head snapped back, blood spurting from suddenly crimson mouth, she slapped him, the forces of the open-hand pop turning him in summersaults. He kicked out with a bear foot and she grabbed his ankle, her hand working upward to grasp his erect penis, she launched and impaled herself on the phallus howling with dark laughter. He smashed a fist against her jaw and she slumped the man pushing her from his penis. She flew at him fighting him he was growing weaker; again and again she mounted his maleness, only to have him shove her away, each shove less forceful tan the preceding one. Then shrieking her taunting laughter she lunged at him and wailed her delight as the phallus drove to the inner depths of her. Fir what seemed like hours the couple fucked their Way across trackless worlds of time. Always in slow circle, until their combined juices were leaking from her, leaving a trail as bright as the milky way the young couple, frozen in voyeurism earth locked they could see that the man was nearly dead with one last supreme burst of courage and strength the man threw out his arms, snagging something out of the maze of clothing and equipment that encircled the couple. The object seemed to fire from his hand through the years straight toward the young man and the woman sitting on the ground in Canada. Nadia screamed. Sam ducked they both jumped to their feet, looking around them. All was still and peaceful. Sam looked at the gun in his hand. He threw the gun at you," Nadia whispered and something else but how?" I think when we finally learn that Nadia…… we'll be dead." You know now what you have to do at Falcon House, don't you?" she asked him I think I've known all along. It's.

Chapter Twelve

"It's Bart, he wants to know how come the phones are still working when everybody else's don't. "

"They don't work in Wheatfield," Balloon replied.

"He says then maybe you would be so kind as to explain how it is he is talking with me on the phone when no one else phone is working."

"Just tell him to think about it... Tithe answer will come to him real soon, hang up the phone and come over here and sit on the couch," Balloon said, Jane went over to the couch and was in front of the only man she had ever loved, she smiled at the misty face and said," all right Sam I will be able to protect you through most of what will occur during the coming says but in the end it will have to be your strength and courage that will see you through."

"May you tell me why?"

"Not yet, most of it you will be able to guess what will happen," she smiled.

"I love question and answer games, none of this is bemusing, Jane!" Balloon fired the thought at her with such intensity it caused her head to ache.

"Sorry," he said, "but enough is enough. "Bart is treating this as some sort of comedy burlesque: John is his usual smart-ass reporter self. Alex angles aren't supposed to talk like that. I 'm not an angle even if I were it wouldn't make any difference. Michael has been known to loose some oaths that caused tidal waves, do you two get along? You and Michael I mean?"

Silence greeted her, "sorry," she muttered "conversing with the spirit world is not something I do everyday you know."

"There you go again being flipped. I May's seem to get through to you; I wonder if any of you know about the horror that is beginning...... For all of you.

"Don't you think we know, Alex?" we live through this. None of you and your deaths, and Jane your death is not going to be pleasant."

"I realize that, Alex, last night I prayed for help I heard you."

"Did he?"

"I am sure he did."

"You don't know!"

"Silence all right knowing Jean Johnson, I 'm sure whatever is in store for me will be of a sexual nature." The mist projected no reply, "Rape, I 'm sure silence am I to be served up for the black mass?" The mist gave no clue Balloon's unblinking eyes could not be read and then she knew what was in store for her. The culmination of awfulness preceding the final hours of hideousness she put her hands over her face and wept. Balloon could do nothing except silently watched and invisibly weep with her. Agential rain began to fall over Wheatfield. "Let's go see this hole in the ground. See the Beasts."

She grabbed his arm "why did you say beasts?"

"Because I know, now but they are the Devil's beasts. My dad fought them or some like them inform County. And now I have to do the same thing. I know now for certain that I have been tapped and chosen.

"If you will pick up where your dad left off. Just, another part of the county that's all. And Roma, Falcon, Tom all those at the house? She asked, almost running to keep pace with his long strides.

"I have to kill them, Sam said!"

"Or try," she was forced to add,

Then they were at the hole in the earth, the ungodly fumes pouring from the blackness hundreds of feet deep almost making them get physically I 'll.'Bastards, Sam said his voice low and powerful. "I know you're there." A growl ripped from the darkness. Sam tossed his jacket to the ground, opening his shirt, exposing the angry Red Cross burned into his skin. The growling intensified becoming louder as others joined in, swelling The howling and snarling to a fever pitch. Sam pulled the 45. From his belt.

"Why don't t you come out?" he challenged them. Let the light touch you but nothing appeared at the mouth of the stinking lair of the beasts, only more howling snarling sprang from the filthy cave. Sam ignored the tugging at his sleeve.

Nadia was so frightened she was trembling. "Come on up" Sam said "let me see you, show me your evil red eyes." How did I know that their eyes were red? And one beast did just that. A young beast that lacked the caution of age leaped forward, just a few feet from the cave opening. It roared at the tall young man it was if history was repeating itself, like father like son. It's breath stinking, Sam shot it right among the eyes, then stood smiling as the dead creature tumbled backward, falling with a boneless thud onto the first level of many tried. Burrow, it would not be wasted its relatives would feast on the cooling flesh and still-warm blood, sucking the marrow from the bones. "One less," Sam said then spat contemptuously on the ground, unaware his father had done and said the same thing years before, 16,000 miles from the west. This time Sam allowed Nadia to pull him away from the rancid hole, leading him toward the house. After the young couple had gone, a huge old beast stuck his head out of the den. He had been on this earth for many hundreds of years and had lived through purge after purge from both human and elements he was old a. He shook his great scarred head and snarled deep in his chest he had never known a human without fear of his kind until now. And that primal sense of warning stuck a resonant cord within his tiny brain. The beast did not distinguish among good and evil; he served his God because ....Well it was the thing to do. He did not have intelligent to question right or wrong. But he did understand courage and something else: fear. And what he now felt was fear, and he did understand why. Growling, the beast slipped back into the earth he must warn the others of this human tell them to stay away. For this human was not like other humans.

This human had been touched by the other side. And the beast feared the other side.

Ohm and Susan spun as the echo of the shot drifted through the timber,

"That was close," 'Susan said but Tom only smiled at her. Back at Falcon house, Roma studied Falcon, as the man stood speaking with Linda he could be so charming at times when he wanted to be, she wondered how long it would take before he got Linda clothes off, not very long if she knew Falcon and she knew him very well. She would like to be there when he spread the girl's legs and filled her with his enormous erection. Roma would like to hear her screaming a thin line of perspiration broke from the skin on her upper lip at just the thought of sex. Damn that young man she couldn't get him off her mind. Roma, knew with a mother's sixth sense, that Nadia had slept with Balloon's bastard.....which was fine, no harm in that, but what Roma did not want was some picky, little holy child to spring from their mating. That would be the height of humiliation a door slammed, and Roma looked around as Tom and Susan strolled in. The girl looked rumpled so her son had made it with the cunt. That was good better than his usual tastes: boys although the Master did not object to his subject engaging in sex with the same gender. Roma noticed Susan now wore the medallion of the master outside her shirt. Very food Tom. Falcon will want to sample her wares as well how nice of you to break her in. She watched Susan touch her son's arm, smile up at him, then walk towards the steps to her quarters. Tom came to his mother's side. "All went well, I see"

. "Very well, mother. But we did hear a shot a few moments ago.

"Oh,'

"Yes. Seemed to come from around the circles of course. Sam would be armed; he is his father's son. "

"Any ideas as to what prompted the gunfire?"

"He probably fires at a beast." They wouldn't have attacked Nadia present.

A frown creased her brow. Unless....she let the unimaginable trail off unless......"

"What mother?

"She became a Christian," Roma said sourly, "if she did that then that changes things considerably yes. But Alex used to do the same thing back in Wheatfield years ago, he would taunt the beasts. No fear in either father or son. But still could her daughter have been converted so quickly. It was possible if so," Roma smiled, that opened yet another may have worms with more alternatives than ever. Tom looked at his mother but unlike his mother, the young man was very familiar with fear but he dared not tell her of that forbidden emotion as forbidden as true love, she would be furious. Tom had learned as a child how to keep his thoughts to himself-blocked so she couldn't read them. But Roma, picked up disturbing vibes from her son.

"What's wrong Tom?" Dark eyes met and held with hers breaking off his gaze under her look.

He shook his head "nothing, mother." He hoped he sounded convincing enough, he didn't but Roma said nothing about it.

"Tom, we have one mission here on earth, and nothing must stand in our way of completing out mission. Do you understand Tom?"

" Yes mother."

Scheming little bastard, Roma thought now you're added lying to your list. Our master wants more converts, more churches.

"It is a very daring move they are taking Wheatfield so soon after failure. If all succeeds it will mean an entire town everyone worshipping the Prince of Darkness. That hasn't happened here on earth in more than so man years that I May's recall the years. Nothing must stand in our way."

"Yes mother. But why simultaneously? Why here and in Wheatfield concurrently.

"Balloon dear, both of them."

"But Alex Balloon is dead mother he is of the other side he cannot be killed again."

She took his arm and guided him into the study, motioning him to sit.

"Tom, understand something. Dear Balloon is very close to being chosen by ....him." She gestured upward with a carefully manicured finger. "Chosen to sit with him."

"God likes his warriors" Tom said.

"That's correct but we don't want that to happen why?" Roma signed sometimes she felt she had birthed an idiot. "If for no other reason son, to humiliated him, to show him he is not inflammable. "Her son nodded his head, narrowing his eyes, "you think Balloon will show up here?"

"Not necessarily, we'd rather he wouldn't, you see if he stays in Wheatfield the temptation to help his darling beloved Jane that simpering little cunt will be even more overpowering ."

"I see." Tom's reply was slow "and if Balloon tries to interfere, he will lose his seat beside God: come under much discover."

"Marvelous, Tom," his mother's reply was edged with sarcasm. "There is hope for you yet."

The look the son gave his mother was laced with hate. "I 'm not a fool, mother'"

"You'll be worse than a fool should you attempt to plot further against me," Roma thought. But her eyes remained cool "I never suggest you were, Tom you're just young that's all."

Tom blinked, and then vanished from the couch, to materialize in his room, how unimpressive, Roma thought. Her thoughts many, she had wondered if you was that naïve at his age?" she ruefully confessed that it was difficult to remember at that age, Louise XI was king of France and Columbus had a few years to go before conning the queen out of her jewels and probably some pussy, Roma thrust her eyes upstairs to her son's room, grimacing as she watched him sitting in a chair rubbing his shins. The fool had banged his legs when he materialized this will have to be my coup de grace, she realized, not without some sadness, I am more than five hundred years old, I am tired, I have been everything from a whore to a nun; the former, If I may pull this off I will have assured myself a place by the smoking side of my master. If I may somehow impregnate with Sam's seed, without cheating too much, and If Nadia is a Christian and Falcon may leave his seed within her, then we may leave the finest demons ever to walk the face of the earth.

"Yes," the heavy voice cut-into her thoughts "that would please me very much and it would assure a place besides me."

Roma stiffened asking "how long have you been listening?"

"Long enough to realize that your son is a fool, your son is not Balloon's bustard "

"You know my son schemes against me?"

"My how the plot thickens" the devil howled with dark, burning laughter"

The Lord of flies grew silent and the room became warm. "You're too old to be thinking about birthing any more children, you years ahead of you here on earth to serve me. You know to birth a demon at your age, what it would mean death. It is written, and Witch, remember this there is no guarantee the demon would live!" Roma said "It would live if you took a hand in it."

"Impossible!"

"You mean you have given your word?" The question was put Sarcastically.

The lord of foulness chuckled, "not necessarily."

"So it is possible?"

"All things are possible, Roma, Nydia, Victoria, Adore Zen Ulrika Willa, Toni, Sibyl have I left any names out that you go by."

"Several" she said dryly, knowing the master was r reminding her of her age.

" all right Roma, but what assurances do I have that you and Falcon will produce one of our own and not some simpering praying, pokier Christian child?"

"If you take a hand, it is guaranteed and then t we may produce true demons."

"Nonsense! The last time that happened was more than a hundred years ago, still it would be a coup against him. Would it not?"

"Yes." Just the thought of him irritated the master. "But you know to produce a true demon means excruciating pain, hours of unparallel agony and certain death for the witch."

"I will do it for you master."

"Thank you. Very well it is up to you Roma do you remember the formula?"

"Yes. You can begin I will help as I may."

Roma sat very quietly in the study as the roaring in her head changed from a howling. Burning cacophony to a rush of colors; finally softening to a muted whisper before dying away. Roma smiled it was settled, she went in search of the book.

In Sam's room, either young person was surprised to see a large canvass covered objected lying on the bed, want to bet I May's tell what's in the canvass? Sam asked.

He opened the canvass pouch, a World War I issue .45. Caliber Thompson submachine gun. A fully loaded drum and three fully loaded clips lay besides the weapon a dozen boxes of 45.caliber Ammunition made up the complete of lethal armament.

"Sam?"

"Don't ask I May's answer your question."

"But you know as well as I where it came from, your dad.." Sam glanced at her while one hand rested on the old powerful Thompson. "God likes his warriors. Dad was a warrior he would have had warrior friends, he would want his warriors where he is and like it or not I guess I 'm a warrior."

"That gives me an aerie feeling."

"I hate to tell you what it gives me."

She read his thoughts. "Sam! Don't be sacrilegious."

He grinned boyishly "I 'm not just telling the truth she blush, ten gestured upward. I'm not too certain what he would think about you having the shit over a job, you've been chosen to do by him I 'm sure he knows the feeling Nadia. He made man in his imagine."

"You're very lovely young lady," Falcon told Julie. Smiling down at her "I cannot imagined why the young men aren't chasing after you" he could not rest the feeling that this lady was hiding something are you really interested in knowing, Falcon?" of course she smiled as she noticed he was looking at derris. She turned walking slowly back to Falcon. They practice Devil Worship...

His laughter seemed out of place. "Oh, my dear did he run that line on you, that's the oldest line in the book, and I do believe that you felt for it,"

"You mean he was playing a joke." Her eyes narrowed, "you mean you don't practice Devil Worshiping?"

"oh heavens no!' Falcon inwardly cringed at the hated word,

Hoping his master would forgive him.

Falcon chuckled and put his arms around her gently pulling her to him she rather liked the feel of the older man. Everything was going as plan she pressed her face against the soft cloth of his smoking jacket, savoring the scent of his cologne; Falcon was equally enjoying the feel of the lush young lady against him. The feel of young breasts; the slight heat from her loins, through centuries of practice he kept his penis soft. "Oh, yes dear just a joke. Oh, we'll have a fine time, you and I . It will be our little secret, right up to culmination."

"The culmination?"

"The height of it all dear," he smiled, his dark eyes glowing with hidden fire, "when we achieve the final summit of course," Julie breathed,

Falcon said. "There was something very disturbing about this young lady."

After Julie had left the library, Roma appeared in the doorway. "Well , Falcon it looks like you have assured yourself a place among her lovely legs."

"But what about the others?"

"All in due time Roma."

"I have missed you for several hours, where have you been,"

"Why I have been speaking with someone who is not of this world." They both could smell the odor of burning sulfur, but it seem to get stronger by mid afternoon the storm had struck, sending all its fury across the land: walls of rain hurled against the great house, the wind bending the trees in a grotesque dance of the element the trees the silver liquid bullets of the heavens hammered against the house. The storm intensified as Roma picked up the huge black book and began reading. No mortal could have held the book's weight no ten mortals could have held it for the black bound book contained the names of every name from beginning of time. Falcon's face was dark with fury and concern for the witch. "I cannot believe you are really contemplating this!"

" It need not concern you." Her reply was cold your participation is minimal.

"Everything you do concerns me. Don't you realize this could well be your Gotterdammerung?"

She shook her head. "Nothing quiet that dramatic, I assure you. That is still in the Future. But if you mean my death yes, I know that."

"And still you persist?"

"For our Master, yes."

" I will try to be there at the end, to help in whatever manner I may. No. That cannot be you have never read the instruction?"

He shrugged, "why should I ?" birthing a demon is not the forte of a Warlock, only those women who are as we may be present, but you may help in the preparation. Tell me what you want me what I must do. I need the blood of a non-believer, that is where we must start Falcon signed, walking to her taking her hand. I am really quiet fond of you Roma she jerked her hand from his don't become maudlin you know the only love we can experience is that which we feel for the master yes. But, I see now why you are doing this thing; she looked up at him 'you fell in love with Balloon, didn't you?" Her steady gaze did not wavier you don't have to go this extreme in penitence, Roma. It wasn't that terrible a deed. It isn't atonement Falcon, out that out of your mind I merely wish to leave a legacy, some part of me. Say it all Ramp, he urged her share it with me our feelings, she shook her head. No. That is past that's not what I mean, and the thoughts of the witch and warlock were mingled. .

"What if we fail here at Falcon house? What if all the plans of the master come to naught? What then?"

"I must say it," Falcon said, "you believe there is a chance we will fail?"

"Balloon's love child has powers even he doesn't know about yet. The young man might never have to bring them into play, yes he could beat us, so any demon child we produce is simply insurance against the future. I have the master's permission to do this, so it is settled and you will have to play a part with Nadia, we don't know she is a Christian."

I Falcon then nodded his head. "I will do my part."

"Always remembering that right up to the last moment we must attempt to convert what we may just in case. I need the blood, the nonbeliever must not die, for we will have to return and again."

Their thoughts were shared, "Yes." Roma said. "She will touch her neck tonight, Falcon."

"Do it." He vanished everlasting life, eternal youth: beauty for the women, never failing virility for men; an orgy that would span time; end to the mundane worries those plaque mortals. That is what the lord of darkness had promised the coven members of Wheatfield in return for their pledge of services to him. For a nether world here on God's earth. Just one spot that would truly be the Kingdom of he damned of the cloven hoof. Then as time trudged on, the disciples of the Mephistopheles could spread slowly outward carrying the message born in the smoking pits to others, until the Prince of Filth ruled a county a state a country, or a world.

All was ready. The, town of Wheatfield no longer held any trace of the Lord God: the crosses were hanging upside down: the alters were draped in black; the instruments of Holy Communion were filled with the vilest of liquids. All was ready to receive the Prince of Darkness. The word was received. Let it begin. Falcon slipped down the quiet hall of the great house pausing often to listen. But any slight sound he might have made was muted by the clashing of the storm as it battered the land.

He paused at a bedroom door, he tried the door knob, unlocked he eased the door open, and let his eyes play across the form of the girl sprawled in a deep sleep on the bed. Judy was a true Christian, Tom had said, loyal to her God and his teaching. She won't be long, Falcon smiled the lips pulling back in a grisly leer exposing the true direction of his long , bloody, life. Fangs now marred the perfection of his Ivory smile; his tongue was swollen, crimson as it throbbed with anticipation mentally savoring the hot burst of living blood. Falcon, slipped into the room, quietly closing the door behind him the noise of the heavy storm covering his soft footsteps, standing over the bed he began a low incantation his deep voice soothing the young woman edging her deeper into sleep the slumber becoming a state of deep hypnosis as his voice touched her dulling senses. Falcon pushed her through the stages of induced sleep, until finally she was secure in the deep somnambulistic state of controlled sleep, and then into sleep that is controlled by the master of the black arts, ruler of the Netherworld. . Falcon, gently slipped the thin cover from her body, licking his lips at the sight of her young beauty, his blood-red tongue bumping over the fangs arousing the engorged organ. Judy was a dark-haired young beauty, the dark brown hair spilling over the pillow shining with cleanliness and health. Falcon touched the silkiness of youth, entwining his fingers in the strands, loving the feel of her. For a moment he sat on the edge of the bed, a dozen emotions playing within his head, he recalled through the years that he had once the same in Spain, centuries ago, with a lovely young lady who had a calling to be a nun she had slept in magnificent villa on the coast while Falcon had toyed with her, finally taking her. He smiled at the thought of that time long ago. Judy lay on her side, clad only in the scantiest of bra and panties, the young ladies now,

Falcon noted no matter how pristine they pretend to be, do enjoy the loveliest of undergarments, he touched the softness of inner-thighs, and the young woman stirred at his touch sighing above the noise of the raging storm stirring in her sleep. Falcon whispered a soothing phrase and she turned onto her back, her legs parting he flipped the front clasp to her lacy bra and young breasts sprang free firm and rose-tipped slightly erect from the rush of cool air. Lovely, Falcon breathed.

He bent his head, and swollen tongue to touch one nipple, working at the tautness. She moved under the tongue play, her small hands clenching into fist at her side. He moved his mouth downward among the young breasts, licking down her stomach, to the slight mound of her lover belly. He rolled the brief panties from her, past the edge of pubic hair, uncovering the sweetness of her moons venires. Bending his head, Falcon tasted the freshness of youth, his swelling protruding tongue dipping into the sudden moisture of her. He pulled away before his sensuality became too great to be controlled and he would have been forced to mount the sleeping beauty. That would have to wait but it would happen again a smile played a macabre dance on his lips perhaps, soon he could mount her as he slipped her life's blood both of them climaxing just as life left her, just at that moment when her heart convulsed and died. That was one of Falcon's greatest thrills and it occurred only too rarely, Falcon, put his hand on her soft belly, allowing his fingers to slide downward to gently caress the mound of Venus, one finger softly parting and entering the folds of her. She moaned under the digital intrusion, and falcon placed his mouth to hers, her breath hot and sweet as she experience a burst of lascivious pleasure her juices wetting her thighs. In approaching climax Falcon's finger en-counting no resistance of maidenhead as it plunged deeper into the satin heat of female. He sensed she was very close to climax. As her knees came up, and her soft rubbing the hard erectile of the vulva, swollen now in sexual enjoyment. Just as Judy began to shiver in the throes of a first climax Falcon, dipped his mouth to her neck and worked his fangs into the carotid artery just behind her ear. For a moment he greedily sucked at the flow of warm blood from her., thrashing body. The liquid, thick and rich, filled his mouth and dribbled down his thirsty throat, the warm slightly salty taste enriching him, flooding him with vitality. He removed a vial from his pocket and held it against Judy's neck, beneath his teeth filing the small bottle with blood she gasped as climax lunged through her, then signed as the warm aftermath filled her with lingering contentment. Falcon eased his fangs from her neck licking away the last drops of crimson from the closing puncture wounds. He removed his finger from her and dressed her, as he had found her, covering her with the sheet. The storm raged on, " sleep well my dear." Falcon said. "For you are now one of us, whether you will remain as such only time will tell, but I shall be back ." He returned to Roma to give the first of many ingredients and to satisfy the aching in his loins. The storm beat on as the witch and the warlock coupled. Roma screaming out a mixture of pain and pleasure as she was impaled on Falcon's huge erection and while Sam and Nadia slept in each others arms content if not safe, and Judy slowly drifted out of her hypnotic state dreaming of being tired, Peter kneeled in front of Lane's nakedness and took pleasure, homosexual love. Lana slept soundly a slight smile on her lips. Linda dreamed of eternal youth and beauty, a dream she often materialized in sleep. Chad, and Tom took their pleasure with Alice and Tonya, Barbara Daisy, a chain of debauchery as the storm raged. Tom caressed the nakedness of Susan prior to mounting her, her cries of pain pleasure filling the room as Tom's manhood filled her. And in the caves beneath the land behind the great house the beasts waited. The storm did not disturb them: they knew they had nothing to fear from the elements it was what walked above them about that they must be wary of. Johnny sat in a chair in his living quarters above the garage and slowly masturbated his thoughts of Nadia. He fantasized of having sex with her all sort of ways from normal to bazaar, he spilled his semen on the floor and leaned back in the chair he felt better, but, it was not enough self abuse, never is the time was growing near, and Johnny wanted real sex, warm blood, Nadia's blood. He rose from the chair, zipping up his pants, letting himself out of the room he slipped through the dark afternoon perhaps he could not have the daughter of the witch this day but there was always one of the others and if he could not have one of the young women there was always one of the young men. Falcon had promised him in a manner of speaking he could take one of the young men.

Chapter Thirteen

Had gathered on the front yard staring at her house, The five of them stood in silence, staring she turned to look at the mist that was Alex Balloon? "Why are they waiting?" for instruction," Balloon projected.

"From Satan? Yes."

"The others will be all right, Alex?

"Yes those at Bart's house the golem will protect them but they will have help and they will."

"The golem May's be destroyed?"

"Not by mortal, not this one only by God?"

"Yes. How is that possible?"

"The golem is earth, he is air, he is water. God made all things, how is it possible to destroy something that God made without his permission?

"We seem to be doing quiet well with pollution and nuclear proliferation the answer is contained within your statement."

"I see."

"No, you don't but you will."

"I'll have to be very strong won't I?"

"Stronger than you have ever been before. The Prince of Filth will test your faith. He will tell you he will stop the pain the degradation the humiliation if only you will renounce your faith in God and he will not be lying it will be terribly, painful won't it Alex?"

" I cannot not lie. Yes. But others have endured it yes. And so shall you." Jane folded her arms under her breasts and turned her attention to the street. A crowd had gathered with the Greens family leading the rabble. "They're coming."

"Yes what must I do?

"Let them attempt to take you. And then?"

"They will discover the awesome power of the Almighty."

"Through you?"

"Yes he could stop all this couldn't he? With one gesture of his hand. Then why doesn't he?"

"Jane he gave them a brain, the power to think, to reason and he gave them compassion if they will but use it. He gave them everything all things to create a world of good, it is up to humankind to decide which path they will take.

"Hey, Bitch!" the harsh voice rang from the yard "I got about nine inches I'd like to shove up your ass just to listen to you holler hey, Jane."

Toni's voice rang "out how about coming out and having some fun, with me and my buddies?"

"How may one man change so?" Jane muttered

"very easily Balloon interjected. The Dark One offers much to those who are less to begin with. A caste system in heavens really Alex!"

"step out on the porch, Jane." Balloon told her, " let them see you are not afraid.

"But I am afraid you are afraid of what confronts you now." Jane opened the door and stepped onto porch, she looked at Steve and Ian. "What do you want,?"

"Some of your pussy, baby." He stepped up grabbing her arms. Steve recoiled backward his face on fire the bubbling and popping of burning flesh filling the late afternoon air. He began screaming running from the house dashing into the road where he tripped on the curb and fell into the gutter, to lay screaming out his life as the fire intensified his head engulfed in flames.

"You like the fire of your master?" Balloon's heavy voice cut through the afternoon. "Then enjoy it. Here let me introduced you to God's power." A woman erupted in flames her body seeming to explode; a man standing besides her suddenly found his feet on fire the flames spreading upward engulfing him. The man and woman ran blindly down the street howling in pain they fell Heavily on the cement as they felt the pain of their brain cooking their wails soon diminished into low moans as life began to leave them. Steve Green had all ready passed into the misty veil, slipping through the wind sighing as he met his Dark Master's world. "Whores and Bastards!" Balloon's voice sent waves of fear through the panicked crowd. "Leave get, out!" they needed no further urging they ran in all directions, Tony lead the pack. The Devil's spokeswoman Jean had known anything like this could happen they ran to her and Tempter watched all that was happening, watched it glumly he simply could not believe his enemy had bestowed so much power in Balloon.

"That was not at all like him surely he did not believe that simpering whore Jane was worth all this?"

"Unless" the Dark One pondered, "unless he knew she would meet the challenge at the end."

"No!" the Ruler of the Netherlands world rejected that. No. not even he would go so far or would he?" He shifted his never-closing eyes to the house of the Jew. " If that dam-able lump of clay was with life and breath from that meddler in the sky that would be an insult, just too great for him to tolerate Satan saw half of what was once a human member of his coven go flying through the air the torso, leaking blood and intestines and organs. The golem stood like a massive fortress in the center of the yard: a sentry against the forces of evil. The golem held one of Satan's people in one huge hand. Then with no more effort than was required to open an envelope, the golem ripped off both arms and sent them flying across the street where they smashed through a picture window the armless body screamed and flopped on the sidewalk, the thick crimson gushing from empty arm sockets he lay squalling in helpless agony Satan's forces scattered in fear and blind panic. The golem lumbered slowly up the walkway and sat on the porch a giant gray man, without features without emotion here only to serve God's people. "You son of a cosmic whore!" Satan scream his message to the Firmament "we made a deal after Prague."

"I make no deals with you Lord of all that is evil." The silent voice filled the sky heard only the demon of all demons.

"Why for these five people? Why not in Israel?"

"The people of Israel may take care of themselves as the world is rapidly discovering, and how do you know I haven't helped there?"

But Satan was in no mood for question and answers. "All bets are off, you son of a Bitch! We agreed twenty years ago on this very spot that I would leave Balloons Bastards to their own wiles in return you would leave me this miserable village, you lied!"

"I do not recall any such agreement." And while Satan howled and screamed his outrage at this supposed trickery on the part of God the almighty brooded amid the thousands of worlds under his command. Had he placed too much on the young man mature enough to victoriously fight the odds against him? . All right he had done all he could do. Far more than he ordinarily did. It was time to withdraw, to think because there was the matter of his mighty ageless warrior who was becoming restless, anticipating a fight among good and evil on earth and wanting very much to be part in any upcoming confrontation. There was that to think about. The black mass that starts the ordeal will begin tonight" Sam said staring at Nadia. " Both here and in Wheatfield"

She stirred in his arms, "how do you know that?

"I just know," Sam replied in a whisper as they lay on the bed in Sam's room listening to the howl and rage of the storm as it slammed the mansion they were fully clothed, and had not made love that day. The impact of the knowledge that they were half brother and sister had finally hit home sobering them and some extent frightening them.

"Your father told you? She asked.

Sam's reply was a long time coming when he did speak his voice was hushed. "One of them."

Johnny slipped through the huge house, knowing he was deluding no one of his kind, and knowing that in all probability, he would be stopped before he could culminate his mission but he had to try for the urges rearing up in the hall. Peeking through the crack in the drapes he watched Balloon's bastard son walk down the hall, past him and into the stairwell leading downward. He listened to the footfall until they faded quickly Johnny shuffled to Nadia's door. He stood listening for a moment hearing the young beauty humming a soft tune. His erection was throbbing his groin aching, his tongue swollen as he placed his hand on the doorknob and gently turned the brass. Nadia was naked all her beauty exposed to Johnny, full mature breasts rose tipped the heavy bush among her legs he could not see her face for it was turned from him. Johnny, pushed the door open a bit farther ready to step inside and take her, by force if necessary when a hand fell on his shoulder, hauling him out of the door, the door closing soundlessly behind him, the loveliness cut off from view. Johnny turned too looked into the fathomless eyes of Falcon, "not her" the tall man whispered" never her Johnny not unless you wish to die ten thousand agonizing deaths a year for all eternity." Johnny dared to argue so great was his need, "she is one of his now, what different does it makes?"

"Fool!" Falcon hissed at him leading the man from the door down the hall "your master has other plans for her and they do not include you. Now leave this wing immediately and do not return ever without orders from Roma or me, Go!" He watched as Johnny shuffled off, his shoulders slumped in rejection. The man was becoming more and more a buffoon, his useless almost past. Falcon could not understand why Roma kept him alive and then Falcon Chuckled without mirth of course he was the last reminder of her love for Balloon. How typically female his eyes narrowed as the thought as the though of the girl behind the closed door entered his mind Falcon could understand Johnny's desire for Nadia was of astonishing beauty and very worthy of any man's attention even Falcon had entertained thoughts of entering her, fantasizing of her moaning beneath him as he gave her more cock than any mortal could ever possess and now he had that permission to do just that but only when Roma gave the word, his smile became a thing of ugliness as he thought of the girl's satin-smooth flesh all hot beneath him he abruptly turned away slipping quietly down the hall then up the stairs to his rooms. There he began to dress for the mass that evening. Once the mass was under way and the true master was called no one would be allowed to leave the area and only those who practiced the black arts could enter, Falcon house and the area surrounding it would be as unattainable as a lost planet in a black hole of space and then Falcon smiled hefting his penis the party could really begin.

" we have no virgins for the ceremony." Roma said as she prepared to dress for the mass.

" Lana," Falcon corrected, "she has never been penetrated.

" I an hesitant to use her," Roma said slipping out of her gown, standing naked in the room. "There is something about her that disturbs me."

"Yes, "Falcon agreed "I picked up on the same troublesome vibes. Pity she is very pretty." Falcon thought no more of it. For the heating in his groin and a slight stirring of the massive organ that hung among his legs. Like Roma, he too was naked very carefully choosing his robes for the ceremony.

"We May's use Judy," Roma mused,

"She is now one of us and I will need more blood from her,"

"The pretty little Linda then,"

"I think not," Roma replied glancing at the clock on the dresser their eyes Met in reflection from the mirror. Their mouths smiled "she thinks she is fooling us you know?"

"Yes" Falcon agreed with a smile "but we know what she is, we'll let her play her little game." Falcon looked at the witch, thinking how beautiful she still was and how desirable he stroked his penis, feeling it filled with hot blood under his touch. Roma laughed at him.

"Contain yourself, Falcon sometimes I believe your brain is in your cock.

Chapter Fourteenth

Coven had gathered amid the circle of dark stones, the worshipers of the Dark One had silently grouped the servants including Johnny. The five men and five women who wished to serve a new master; Roma and Falcon and Tom and Howard stood naked inside the inner circle, his eyes glazed from the drugs in his system, the torch light reflected dully from the scarcely comprehending eyes of the young man outside the circle of people the beasts had gathered quietly more than a dozen of them. They stood patiently slobber leaking from massive jaws their eyes glowing red with evil anticipation. For they knew that someone died at the mass and they would feast tonight. Roma went amid the new members cutting off a small piece of their hair from each head, and then she walked to a stone where the book rested. Their names were carefully recorded in that evil book, the hair placed besides the name just as we have done for hundreds of years, Roma silently mused as I personally have done for than five hundred years, and those before me for thousands of years all the way back to the caves and beyond before the first blood, Roma cut her eyes to Howard's nakedness as a feeling of something very amiss struck her something was wrong, Falcon sensed it as well, walking swiftly to her side. "What's wrong?" he asked his voice low

"The master is here and he is angry."

"What about?"

"I don't know."

The voice of the Ruler of the Netherworld boomed in their heads, thundering to them in a roar only they could hear. "Is this the best you may do? One shivering male?" Roma thrust her thoughts to the Ruler of Hell. "We did not think you would object."

"You did not think!" Satan roared, causing them both to cringe, "that much is correct, look at your idiot son, Roma. Look at him stroking his organ practically drooling at the mouth like a beast as he thinks about a man love disgusting and the son that should have been mine is crouched not a thousand meters from the circle, watching with your daughter the daughter that should be taking part in the ceremony worshiping me ! You have failed again. Woolley warned me you had a streak to be sure but nevertheless there what in the name is unholy have I ever done to deserve you two? This should be easy. The world is spinning about in utter chaos, wars breaking out everywhere morals finally decline at a satisfying rate of deterioration; drugs and free sex and oh, for pity 's sake do I have to lecture the both of you? Now you hear me well, witch and warlock the both of you will not fail this time, these are my commands you will established a coven on these grounds to insure that I have ordered more memories into reinforce this group. . They will be here tonight. you Roma will give me a demon son from the seed of Balloon's bastard, you Falcon will give me a Bitch demon from the womb of Nadia but test them before you seduced them as God is doing, see if they are worthy of my touch, you must offer them ample opportunity to leave and allow them to do so if that is their choice of course," the Devil chuckled, "you may ambush them on their way out." The torches smoked for a few moments the circle of stones silent in flickering light then Satan roared, "don't either of you really think I care how you accomplish any of this . I put the sacrifice business in the mind of that fool writer a thousand years ago. It's been repeated ever since. Why is everything I say constantly taken out of context? May's I make a joke occasionally? After all, I was once an angel and a god dammed good one, if I must say so, myself I 'm not humorless I gave the world Pilate, Hitler, and rock and roll music didn't I ? no Roma Falcon you will not fail me , I want to hear the screaming of those pokier holy people I want to hear the wailing as there blood stains the ground and I want to see a demon burst from your womb and matching bitch from the cunt of your Christians daughter. There are no rules none! I have this precognition that I am going to be defeated in Wheatfield very well I may live with that; I may accept it. I will deserve some satisfaction from it however, the wailing and begging of Balloon's Christians whore as she is ravaged and flogged and finally nailed naked to the cross and no you can not fear Balloon, we will not interfere here, he'll be much too busy back in Wheatfield from the firmament, he broke his word even though he denies it so I see no need for many rules you two hear me well; I want blood, pain degradation filth everything we believe in and more, tell your fool son to mount the male if that is what he wants, he will never be anything other than a stooge to me ,failure. Roma you failed with both your latest children but at least, and it pains me to say this Nadia did accept something she is faithful to something which is much more than may be said of that foolish son of yours he disgusts me, scheming, plotting foolish boy is doubtful. I shall not return until you have completed your assignment I must return west."

"That Psalm singer broke his word, thinks he has me fooled, thinks I believe he has departed well, I don't trust him. I know he's got something up his sleeve I just don't know what. So be careful Balloon's goody-two-shoes son has tremendous powers which is another reason I 'm sending in help, so good-bye and don't fail me!"

"Something happened," Sam whispered "I feel as if I was locked in some kind of time warp where everything stood still."

"Me too" Nadia said returning the whispered look.

"Roma and Falcon are moving now they're speaking with Satan."

"How do you know that?"

"Some, one just told me she looked at him in the darkness her eyes wide and scared who?"

"I don't know." Nadia suddenly gasped "my God!" She grabbed at Sam's arm look at both of them grimaced their shock and horror As Howard was led to the dark altar by two servants and Tom, began sodomy of the young man. Howard screamed his outrage and pain fighting against hands that held Him while Tom laughed as he forced the ugliness Howard screamed again his cries echoing around the small valley. Roma ran to the scene of the rape her black robe open, exposing her nakedness the stones preventing Sam and Nadia from seeing what was taking place they could but wonder what the witch was doing kneeling in front of the altar, Roma sank her teeth into the femoral artery of Howard's thigh the blood gushing from the fang bites spilling over her face and lips she drank greedily of the hot red liquid biting him again and again working steadily upward until his thigh and groin area were pricked with needles marks. She drew away from him her face covered with blood. Howard's cries tapered off into low moans as Tom began shivering with approaching climax. The beasts began dancing a grotesque obscene hunching a debasement of any rhythm that needed grace or beauty. Soon all were dancing King of night Lord of flies and of filth hear this one scream for you! Howard screamed as Tom climax. The coven members danced about the altar tearing off their cloths. Howard lay unconscious across the altar. Falcon pointed to the young man draped in humiliation across the flat stone altar. Tend to his needs he ordered Then oblivious to the cold and damp, the men and women coupled like animals their naked bodies gleaming in the torch-lit candle of stones.

Sam and Nadia made it back to the mansion just seconds before the coven members summoned by their master arrived pulling up to Falcon in half a dozen automobiles, and vans the young man and woman stood in their quarters the light out the rooms dark, watching the Devil worshipers leave the vehicles, walking up the steps to the house. Not all of them were willing participants some fought the hands that held them: some were crying a few were a little more than children. Nadia closed the drapes and stood for a moment, Sam's arm around her. "Those poor little girls down there," she sobbed, pressing her face against his chest, crying and trembling with fear finally overcoming for her terror and horror, she pulled away from Sam and turned on The bureau lamp, she looked at the bed gasped, one hand flying to her mouth.

She pointed on the bed and saw that Sam's bible was open. And two chapters circled in red and his beret, his ranger beret he carried with him in his luggage, whenever he traveled, lying besides the bible. Sam it occurred to him in his mind as he accepted the knowledge that was some things that could not be explain so is it. He walked to the bed, looked at his beret, touched it then answered Nadia's yet unasked question "I worked and sweated my butt off to get this, I 'm very proud of it." He touched the red that outlined the chapter in the bible.

"What is it? She asked.

" Blood."

"Who's Blood?

Sam shook his head." I don't know let's read this. They sat on the edge of the bed reading in silence for a few moments trying to comprehend the message contained therein.

"I've never read the bible before." Nadia confessed "except for a few quick peeps at friend's homes. But it sounds absolutely fascinating."

"It is Nadia, I don't understand any of this what does the blood have to do with this?"

"There!" she pointed at a passage, she read loud "and they overcame him by the blood of the lamb. Could that be it?"

"I don't think so I just don't know."

" Mother said that my real father often told her the bible was vague given to many different interpretations, and I saw one of his heads as it were wounded to death; and his deadly wound was healed; and all the world wondered after the beast and they worshiped, the beast, saying who is like unto the beast? Who is able to make war with him?" They both read the remaining verses of the chapter in silence,.

Nadia finally saying. "It could mean so many things, Sam, Michael was a Warrior right?"

"One hell of a warrior"

"Sam!" She gave him a disapproving look for his paradoxical state.

"Anyway warriors fight. Blood is spilled right?"

"Yeah, he confessed reluctantly.

"Could be you're right.. Is the beast the Devil?"

" I guess so,."

"You're a preacher's son, Sam you're supposed to know these things.

"I 'm a backslider, honey not a very good Christian."

She kissed his cheek "I don't believe that Sam. Not for a second. Michael cast out Satan right?"

"That's what it says so of all the angels in heavens, who would be the one most likely to help someone fight the Devil?"

Sam looked at her in the dim light the look he gave her was extreme uncertainly "Are you Nadia saying that Michael is helping me?"

" That he is here maybe he doesn't know Sam maybe he isn't here; maybe he doesn't have to be here, yet to do these things, yet if your father was a warrior who would he most likely make friends with up there?" She pointed upward.

"Honey this is getting a little I bit farfetched when was the last time you recall Angels appearing here on earth?"

"Well how would we know really? I mean people might not want to speak of the sighting right?"

"You have a point."

"Yeah, for fear of being laughed at, I seem to recall reading that Michael did appear to help in some way with Joan of Arc. All right your father had to have appeared to give you that envelope didn't he?

"He's in Wheatfield right now, isn't he?"

"Yeah. But my father isn't an angel."

"How do you know that?"

Sam shrugged "I don't" before either could say another word a light tap sounded on the door. Sam signed heavily and stood. a "put away the bible Nadia, no sense tempting the gods from either end of he spectrum." He opened the door; Roma stood looking at him her dark eyes burning with a strange light. "Mrs. Williams excuse me Roma," Sam corrected, "It's late for a social call, isn't it?

"Oh, I assure you, this is no social call. He smiled. All bets down, the pot's right and time for the last card right?"

She laughed, "oh, my dear you are your father's son. Yes, darling, time for a little chat."

"Among good and evil?"

She shrugged the moment lifting her breasts and she noted that Sam noticed. She had changed low, the v dipping far into the swell of her breasts.

"Good and evil, Sam? Well perhaps tell me how far have you taken my daughter into the candy-coated world of Christianity?"

"I baptized her," Roma grimaced her nose as if she smelled something badly.

"How perfectly disgusting before or after you fucked her?"

Sam stood in the doorway he said nothing Roma smiled "your Christians self proclaimed really want it both ways don't you? You want on one hand to mouth all those heavenly platitudes, but you still want to fuck whenever the mood grips you have you eaten her pussy yet, Sam?"

Sam returned her sardonic smile, sensing she was deliberately baiting him, trying to anger him. She laughed "very good Sam I couldn't bait your father either, who by the way is also Nadia's father and of course Tom's father too. I just thought you might like to know that the next time you got an urge to screw my, my! What would your God have to say about that?"

"I don't know I haven't asked him."

She arched an eyebrow "well how casual you are. That cosmic gnome you Worship might take exception at your flip attitude toward sex."

"We'll take our chances."

Then, without explanation her smile changed to one containing a trace of sadness. "Believe me darling we are all about to do that I see no reason to stand here in the hallway discussing this why don't we behave as civilized human beings." She laughed aloud "at that and adjourn to the den where we may be more comfortable I assure you no harm will be fall you, we do have a great deal to discuss ."

"Mac, Howard,, Janet, Judy, Lana?" Nadia spoke from her seat on the edge of the bed. "They are sleeping soundly Howard on his stomach I should imagine. I have no doubt what you will both rush to their sides upon walking to tell them the dire new isn't Howard one of you now? Sam asked, and wondered how he knew theta perhaps yes.

"You are a wise one aren't you?"

"Of course he is."

"then get him out of Mac's room, bunk him somewhere else give Mac a chance at least." Roma flushed you young man, "do not order me about." Sam slammed the door in her face a short pause, a tap on the door. Roma's anger was under control.

"As I may be that my God will protect me. Against those who serve the beast."

Roma turn her head and spoke in a language that Sam did not recognize when she again faced him, he asked "what language t was that?"

"That was ancient Gallic, I speak all languages known on earth, Sam and many that have long since vanished.

"Considering how ancient you must be, I should imagine that would come in handy."

Roma howled her approbation, "oh, very good, Sam! Score one point for you oh, my, yes you are a most worthy foe. I have instructed that Howard be moved Into a room of his own." She smiled for all the good it will do.

"Mac are you coming to the den?" Sam glanced at Nadia she nodded her head, her face pale.

" Yes." Sam said to the witch. She vanished in front of his eyes without a trace.

"Unusual activity tonight." The astronomer said to his colleagues, his partner in sharing the lonely nights searching the heavens from their earthbound observatory in California "oh what kind of?"

"I don't know that I may explain it" his friend said glancing at him.

"Twenty-five years in this business and you give me an answer like that?"

"Come on, Ralph you may do better than that. I saw quick burst of lights; not connected with anything I know about, strange almost like messages are being sent from deep space."

"You been reading the bible again Ralph?" his friend asked not unkindly, but with a slight sarcastic tone to his voice. It was something his partner had grown used to years before.

"I read the bible everyday, Tim." Tim rose from behind his desk and climbed the ladder to the huge telescope, actually a series of scopes each amplifying the other boosting the power to tremendous dimensions. The agnostics watched the heavens for a few moments, pausing only to check his computation against those of his friends they matched perfectly, verifying the location of the supposed sighting nothing,

"Tim you've been working too hard." that's all Ralph said nothing in reply.

"Did you shoot film?

"You know I did." The reply was softly stated.

"Well let's develop it."

But Ralph was strangely reluctant to do that and that only peaked his colleague's curiosity even further and when questioned he would only shake his Head "all right Ralph," Tim, sat besides his friend, "come on give, we've been friends and co-worker for many , many years." He looked at him closely unlike Tim, Ralph was a Christian or tried to be and he believed in the big bang theory about as much as he believes a duck could fly.

"There won't be anything on the film," he finally said.

"Why?"

"Because what I saw May's be, won't be filmed, that's why so let's change the subject, and get some coffee." Tim put out a restraining hand.

"I won't kid about your belief in God, Ralph. I may sense this is not the time a and I believe you did see something and I stress something, it will not go any further than this platform, I give my word now what did you see?" Ralph's eyes appear deep-sunk in his skull and his face was pale he ran nervous fingers through thinning hair. "I saw the face of God."

Tim sat very quietly for a moment, " all right Ralph is that all?"

"What else? What did he look like? Angry concerned worried, In human form? In a manner of speaking what was he doing? Just skipping around the sky? And I don't mean that in an ugly way."

"He was meeting with someone something another being."

"Ralph! Have you lost your mind? Are you serious?"

" He was well, it looked like he had intercepted someone something a being like I said I've never seen anything like it . Tim it was terrible it was beautiful, wrathful I hate to be redundant, but it was awesome. "

"Explain awesome."

"I don't know that I may. The figure appeared, I don't know exactly." Tim had worked with his friend for too many years to think he was pulling his leg and to not take him seriously. Ralph Woodard was a highly respected man in his field, one of the top men in the world, Constantly in demand for speaking engagements and classroom lectures, something very close to excited fear touched.

He had not experience it in a long time, "go on buddy tell it all."

Somewhere in the vastness of the huge planetarium, a phone began to ring. It rang several times before someone stilled the jangling. Ralph sighed. "It seemed to me that the two figures were, well, arguing. I guess is the right word. Almost violently the one more imposing figure impressive was pointing upward the warrior-appearing figure was pointing downward pointing with that terrible looking weapon he held in his hands." The blinker on the telephone popped on. Tim finally picked up the phone. Yeah?" He listened for a moment his eyes widening. "No warning; nothing?" Impossible!" he listened for a moment longer. All in one night?" This close together?" Good God!" He hung up.

"What?" His friend asked

"Small volcano in Maya Archchipelago just blew its cork. Hell, it's been dormant for centuries. No warning, none"

Ralph smiled. "What else?"

"A couple of small monsoons. A tidal wave or two. All without serious damage, people reporting some sort of heavenly voice coming out of the sky. Their words; damn sure not mine large hail in spots tremendous lighting, reported around Montréal."

"Where around Montreal?"

"Seventy-nine west why?"

"And the temple of God was opened in Heaven," Ralph said, closing his eyes "and there was seen in his temple the ark of his testament and there were lighting, and hail."

" What the hell is that derived, Ralph?"

"Revelation, chapter eleven, verse nineteen It was a fluke of nature,"

"Ralph!

"If that is what you believe,"

"God dam it, Ralph! Now listen to me : you're scientists you know as well as I, that there is a logical explanation for everything. I'm not going to argue fact or fiction with you we've been doing that for a quarter of a century, and all it gets us is out of sorts with each. I 'm going to get that fucking film and see what's on it, I 'all be back shortly ." w h e n Tim returned, Ralph had not moved from his seat. "Nothing"

" I told you there wouldn't be I 'm going to switch scope position, take a look at that new star all right you don't object?"

"Why should I ? maybe your apparition will pop up again don't you want to see your holy people?" Ralph smiled at his friend, the expression on his face was strangely tight.

"News?" Ralph asked.

" Some stargazers up in Canada wanted to know if any of us had witnessed something some vision in the sky tonight, said he didn't want me to think him a fool, or that he'd been boozing on the job but it appeared to be two things arguing."

"And ? Ralph prodded them knowing there was more.

" He said," Tim signed, "that others had called in from reporting stations all around the world said they all witnessed the same whatever it was . said they were all to use his words awestruck "

,"go on Tim."

"You really want to rub my nose in it, don't you?"

"No, old friend, I don't well I didn't ' see it. If I had seen it. I probably would have been able to identify the sighting without falling back up on proven superstition."

The two men glared at each other for a few seconds, Ralph finally breaking the silence "what is it they claim to have seen?" The astronomer stalked from the upper platform, carefully climbing down the ladder level. He walked to the door Behind him. Ralph looked upward, at the stars that twinkled high above him through the open roof. He said in a voice that held the utmost respected, " I never had any doubts . Do you want introduction?"

Chapter Fifteen

Roma, asked the young couple, "I imagine we'll all get to know one another very well before the next eight days are up."

Sam answered the den was crowded with young people, and Sam knew Nadia felt as he did Somewhat edgy and very much alone. The young people, the kids they had seen being forced into the house were not present. Sam supposed they had been drugged and put to bed. Most of the men in the room hard-looking types with craggy faces and savage eyes. The women were attractive, in a sultry, evil way with unreadable eyes. A couple of them were beautiful members of the older covens in this country to the United States,'

Falcon said gesturing at the new group. "Your God broke the rules we saw no reason to maintain our standards."

"Why are you telling us this? Sam asked ?"

" So, you may make your choice, naturally." Falcon replied, "You may live or die the latter being rather hideously, I might add should you foolishly choose that courses."

" The choice has been made for us," Sam said, glancing at Nadia.

"That was yesterday," Roma said, " I assure you both, you can leave this area if you desire."

" Our God would prefer that we remain," Nadia said, the words blurting out of her mouth. Falcon laughed as his eyes mentally undressed the young woman. Of all the female present Nadia was by far the most lovely and desirable and Falcon was looking forward to the moment when he would spread those lovely legs and position himself inside. "My ,Nadia, how brave you have become with your new found religion. Are you looking forward to serving a half a dozen men at one time?"

"I don't believe that time will come, Falcon," she told him.

"We'll see," the reply was spoken softly, filled with menace " Sam don't you see your position is hopeless there is no way out for you, join us,

before it is too late."

" if that is the case then take us now, what are you afraid of ?" Sam asked " The room filled with laughter.' " Afraid?" Roma, said." My dears I 'm not afraid, we'll not afraid, but put that thought out of your mind. If, or when the time arrives, we shall take you. Both by force why risk personal injury I when there is always the chance we may convince you both of you to come over to our side?"

"You will be tempted." Balloon's words came back to his son "and you will fall to some of those temptation."

" Hi, I 'm Terry" one of the young women said . " And I have a question why would you want to resist us ? I don't understand I was once a Christian raised in the church. A few years ago my mother was dying of cancer. I prayed to her God then to save her, spare her, or at least allow her to a long and low horrible death unforgivably agonizing. Don't hand me that bullshit of your God. Yet after I joined the forces of Darkness. My father was struck by a car and lay dying in a hospital I asked our Master to save him and he did." she moved to stand besides her father and grab his crotch, "see he still lives," she said with a gribble..

"Very well, I may assure you both of that we serve our God," Sam said.

"our God serves us double talk." Toni said as she looked at Nadia, open envy in her eyes as she gazed at her beauty. " I hope your man fucks with more conviction than he talks." Nadia's smile was sweet but tingled with hot anger. "Odds are, dear you'll never know you'd better stick to dear old dad." Toni flushed, with anger and rage, moving toward Nadia her fists balled no one made any attempt to stop her. When she got within swinging distance, Nadia, to Sam's surprise gave the young woman a solid shot in the jaw beginning to redden and swell.

" You have discovered," Roma spoke to the room "that my daughter is very capable of taking care of herself." She gave Falcon a very hot look. "Thanks to Falcon, he insisted upon teaching her the rudiments of self-defense when she was a small child."

Falcon had to smile. "Very good , Nadia you remembered well." Nadia rubbed her bruised knuckles and said nothing.

" well?" Roma whirled to glare at Sam, " your decision?"

"We're staying,"

"A decision you will have to live with and regret," Roma said with a smile but thinking all is working out very well the lights went out, [lunging the room into darkness. Nadia screamed in terror and from the firmament the vault of Heavens, a figure ripped toward earth, moving at a speed untraceable by any machine that was ever known to man as the figure from the world behind the veil again it made contact with earth, by the circles of stones behind the home known as Falcon Mansion , a strange unearthly sound was heard and the creatures of the forest and the beasts underground were frozen in motion by the appearance of a near apparition, The figure, huge pale and ghostly made no sound as it walked to the dark circle to sit on one of the dark stones. There ,it appeared to brood for a moment, its eyes like lighted sparklers in the night. But those of his choosing the phantom traveler rose from the rock and turned to look at the great house, its eyes becoming as mysterious as its identity, and mission. The eyes glowed, for a brief time, and then faded into hard tiny bits of diamond white. The traveler turned his back to the dark mansion, shook its great head, and walked toward the darkness of the forest. The ground trembled slightly as the manlike traveler walked, its feet clad in sandals, with leather thongs laced up the legs at the knees. The dark robe was ankle long, belted at the waist with leather. As the ghostly appearing man passed the rock altar, stilled stained with the seamen from the man rape, a sword appeared in one mighty hand. The sword had struck the stone a huge splotch of white appeared, starkly visible in the night, burned forever in the altar stone. The man snorted in disgust,

and then spat on the ground, besides the black alter, the spittle hissing and Sizzling on the earth. And then the cosmic traveler was gone, vanishing as quickly as it came. The voice boomed in Sam's head. "This is your period of testing!" it was voice he had not heard before, and it seemed to be very near him, "you were warned that you would be tempted. Fear not, for the Lord God is with you. Resist all you may, with all your might and do not fear should you sometimes fail, for Christians are not required to be perfect, they are simply forgiven." The voice faded in silence.

"Did you hear that?" Sam questioned Nadia silently.

"No. Hear what?"

"I'll tell you later."

Roma was conscious of something alien in the room, not physically present, but more a mental thrusting and something else crept its way up and down her spin: the first unfamiliar feelings until she had successfully driven them away then stood quietly as her daughter and Sam left the room. She glanced at Falcon. He pushed into her brain, "Did you feel that power a moment ago?"

"Yes. What was it?"

" I don't know I believe," Tom said, speaking for the first time , " that we all should retire for a little fun and games. We have time, for we are many, ands it is only the two of them."

"Fool!" Roma looked at him, knowing, that he would be no match, for Sam Balloon. By all that is unholy, she mused.

Chapter Sixteen

Alex Balloon I love you very much."

" go to sleep." Alex told Jane,

." I have loved you for so long, go too sleep." She started to drift off a little, she could not sleep Jane was trying to prepared herself for the ordeal that lay ahead for her. As, the ever-living vapor wavered by her Balloon projected,

"Oh,' Jane, you do not know how hard I fought to come here; you do not know how difficult it was; and you do not know the horror that awaits you. But I do. And I will suffer, as you suffer and I will be powerless to help until the end. When your times comes, Jane don't fight it; let the life slip from you; let it ebb until I may take a hand and end your suffering. We sinned, Jane. Years ago, just as our son and my daughter have sinned God works strangely, sometimes, my love, and to enter his kingdom is not the easiest or the simplest thing to do. Have strength and faith, my love, for I will be besides you in all your trials and he will be watching us both. I do love you darling, as much as I did in this world of mine, his world, as I did as a mortal." And the mist became a blanket that covered her with gentleness, a love, so pure; it could only come from above.

"We have a full twenty-four hours to gather our strength for the ordeal that will be facing us," Sam said, the words seeming to leap from his mouth as if a separate brain had taken full control.

"Why?" Nadia asked. How do you know that?"

"Someone is telling me these things. And I don't feel inclined to question the source. Sunday is one day the forces of black magic, old Satanists, whatever you choose to call them, May's move, supposedly he put a disclaimer on that.' That's God's day and we'll probably be left alone.." He fell moodily silent for a few moments.

" What are you thinking Sam? I May's quiet read your mind."

"Probably the same as you, how we're going to get out of this mess; how we're going to win it."

"You mean if we're going to win it ." His eyes became alive with a fever she had never before witnessed.

"No, Nadia, not if we May's have any doubt if we're going to win this thing. If we have any doubt all we, might well hang it up.

"I 'm not as strong as you think I am?"

His words were spoken, much more harshly than intended. Tears touched her eyes, rolling down her cheeks," Don't be angry with me please? I 'all do whatever you tell me to do, but you're have to help me." He signed, taking her hands in his "I 'm sorry I snapped at you, honey I 'all die for you if I have to." and she knew in that he meant every word. "I love you Nadia. Even though I know it's wrong, and I 'all, or we'll pay for it someday. I May's deny my love for you anymore than I could deny my love and faith for the Lord God."

"Roma was right, you know our love is wrong, and God won't have it; he won't allow it to go unpunished."

"Let's get out of this.......mess first," he said grimly. "Then we'll worry about t that tomorrow?"

She forced a smile, "but where is Tara; Sam?"

"Whenever we choose to make it honey."

"And we will make it together, promise me ?"

"Yes, I promise." They wanted very much to touch, kiss or something, but she pulled her hands from his and stood, walking across the hall to her room, picking up the bible on the way; I 'm going to study this for a while Sam. He could but nod his head in approbation.

Chapter Seventeen

The crowds of the Devil worshipers in Wheatfield paraded up and down the Greens front yard, shouting filthy words and mailing obscene gestures. But no one dared to violate the space guarded by the huge clay man, and the golem would not venture past the front yard. It was a stand-off. "Around back," Jean suggest to her foreman" we'll keep that firkin monster occupied here; you take some people around to the back of the house. Quietly now. Try to take them alive so we may have some fun with them." Jack nodded his approbation, "Ill get in my truck and pretend like I 'm leaving, that ought to throw them off." Jack, didn't know where the clay man was, he could pop up, and be anywhere. And there he is watching me, he couldn't wait to get his head on Jane, she was a prissy little thing, she was so high and mighty, thinking she was better than any one else, knowing she was fucking the preacher. Alex Balloon, all the time. The two overanxious members of the coven nodded their heads in anxious agreement.. They ran across the yard they made it to the back porches steps before two shotguns blasted, the slugs from one catching boo in the face, blowing his head apart. The other blasted hitting Clint in the center of his chest, flinging him backward He died as he hit the ground, "I didn't figure they was that dumb," Jack said, fingering the medallion that hung around his neck. "Come on. I got an idea." Jean wasn't surprised to hear their attempt to rush the house failed. Things were not going as planned not at all. "what's your idea, Jack?"

"Simple, the foreman said burns them out." Gasoline was found, Molotov cocktails made the first firebomb exploded in the hands of its preparer; the second and third ones bounced off the house and went out. The fourth and fifth bombs were picked up by the clay man and hurled back at the crowd, badly burning one man and blinding another. "Enough!" The Prince of Darkness hurled his command into the brain of Jean. "It is as I thought: useless. Let them be." And the Dark one knew then his attempts to wrestle the town of Wheatfield from the hands of God and build a coven there were doomed to Failure. The Almighty meddler had allowed him to waste his time here for more than thirty years, knowing all along . He would not allow the final act. The Dark one brooded his thoughts more savage than usual he searched the heavens for some sign of his life long foe, but he was not found "could it be, Satan mused could it be true, that he really did retire into his firmament ?" But why would he do such a thing? The Dark One could find no logical reason for such silly behavior on his part. There were reasonably innocent people in this miserable town… well, not really innocent, he amended that but had not so far, interfere with their torture their rape; their degradation.

"Why? Why? Why would he save only the Jew and those silly gentiles?" Satan could not believe, he would allow the torture and rape of Jane, simply to test Alex Balloon…… "Or would he?" no, that might be it in part but there was more to this. The Prince of Rates knew that God sometimes acted in mysterious ways, but this was erratic, even for him. It made no sense. And Satan knew something else, he had to work to hard here to accomplished anything at all, he added "no …. Something was amiss." There had to be more to it for him to behave so, strangely, the Lord of Pus looked upward and roared.' "Star Wart? Answer me you Bastard!" But there was no reply from the firmament. The King of shit howled and screamed his displeasure, vending his anger, fouling the heavens with profanity daring the mighty to give him a reply they had been the first to sense it; for they were much more animal than, human, and could feel with a perception that humans did not possess that it would rain snow, the ground tremble, the sky produced hail and when things were going badly for their kind. Jane looked at the mist that was Alex and asked him "will they come for me this night Alex?"

"No. It will be near the end when they come for you, and they will have me about 36 hours from now, and then it will be over for you on earth."

"And we will leave together?"

"Yes' Bart, Anita, Betty, and Wayne will come with us?"

"Yes."

She rose to get his bible and opened it to one of the chapters in the book of Psalm she had been reading. "I wish it was all over," she said.

"We May's get out!" A coven member told Jean, near hysteria in her voice.

"Everywhere we turn, we're blocked." At her right another member said drunkenly. "We done been where in this part of Wheatfield, down every road we're blocked by what? Jean asked the question. Nothing.'

Nothing Dimmit! That doesn't make any sense what the shit do you mean nothing?"

"There's something there but you May's see it. It's invisible but it's solid like a big bubble you may feel it, but you May's get no purchased on it. And we see two or four out of states drive right through it, but when we run over there it was closed to us. And them people in the cars didn't pay us no mind at all it's like we was invisible, or something that's right" the mayor of Wheatfield said he like the others was filthy his clothing was reeking from sex and sin and death. He was unshaven and his breath and body stank, "we're trapped in here, Wendy, like rats in a barrel, with no way out, what's going on?" he screamed, his fear becoming contagious touching others of he coven.

"Now just calm down" Wendy said, soothing them. "The Master will take care of us. He promised he would; hasn't he always?" so far, they all agreed "All right I'll speak with him. For now, you people relax. Go get one of those not of us and crucify them have some fun. Everything will be all right you'll see." she smiled, and words seemed to placate them, and they went into town, to find another luckless, hapless so-called Christians; they had all had such fun listening to them screaming while they were being tortured by them, raped them nailed them nailed them to the rough made crosses with naked tortured bodies dangling from the towers of pain. The men and women Who still screamed out their lives was dying wondering why..... Just because they had cheated a little but in business here and there; just because they had professed to be Christians, and had secrets. They openly held hate in their hearts, for the black people, Jews, spics, that shouldn't?" just because they had lied in their hearts while they prayed to him, knowing they were lying all the time, that wasn't enough to warrant this was it? Just because they had enjoyed browbeating employees and cheating on income tax and palming a few bucks a day from their employers and every now and then getting in a quick fuck from their neighbor's wife or husband or secretly getting together with the boys to watch a movie.... That wasn't it?" After all, hadn't they gone to church every Sunday, just like the bible instructed them to do. The invisible barrier around Wheatfield and parts of Fork County didn't upset Mephistopheles; there was no barrier he could not penetrate except heavens, and he certainly had no wish to go there. And that he knew he was going to lose in this locale did not bother him very much.... Not really: he had lost before and would again. These ignorant stupid greedily, vain, petty grasping mortals were all his anyway. No matter what took place during their short squirt of breathing life... most of them were too ignorant to understand why he was doing this. It was almost as if he had made up his mind to give up on the human race end the game. But Satan knew that wasn't true known they had a few more years in content ahead of them no. He wasn't yet ready to end the game and sear the world with nuclear fusion. This world the game the foul one knew had many millennia left; other worlds yet to experience his and his warfare thousands of creatures left to yet develop into thinking beings for now, though yet undeveloped enough to make the choice among darkness and light. Truths and lies beauty and ugliness. No, that was not it and then the Dark one decided as he had done so many times in the past, that he really didn't know what motivated him what caused him to accept one human being and rejected another his philosophy was so complicated so simple , Satan corrected His thinking, to make it appear confusing well, the foul one concluded.... So much for Wheatfield. His enemy had won again but his smile was all things evil, there was still Falcon house, and even should I lose there I will not lose entirely for the witch was ready to make her move, to give him a demon child the warlock ready to make his move to give him another demon child, and he had more souls for the pits. So, all in all it had not been an entirely. Fruitless pursuits. No, not at all I 'all leave these fool and twits to their own cunning here in this wretched village. Go to Falcon house; see how I can be of assistance there. There was always tomorrow.

Neither Sam nor Nadia encountered many coven members on this, the Lord 's Day. Those they did see walked with quickly furtive steps shifty hurriedly averted eyes and slumped shoulders as if expecting a sudden blow from behind.

"Sam?" Nadia asked as they had breakfast alone in the large dining room,

"Wouldn't this be the day to defeat them'?

"It would seem so," the young man replied. "But yet. I don't believe the period of testing is over for me." She accepted that without question.

"Why are they so I don't know afraid I guess is the right word?"

"You mean today?" she nodded.

"God's day honey, we're safe comparatively speaking that is but some warning voice a sense I guess, deep inside me, tells me to be on guard for this is their territory, not ours or his,"

Nadia said, "Yes." She looked up, with sudden fear in her eyes.

"What's wrong?"

"Falcon and Roma are coming our way,"

"To hell with them."

" apt. choice of words," she said smiling, the witch and the warlock stopped at the buffet line to fill their plates then walked to the table, Falcon smiling saying I know you young people won't object if we join you. Not at all, Sam returned the smile we were just about to say a morning prayer for thanks. He Pointed upward to him. How disgusting!" Roma said,

"go right ahead" Falcon said," but you will understand if we don't join in? Sam bowed his head and Nadia followed suit, not knowing what the young man was going to do, she didn't even know if Sam knew a morning prayer of thanks. Sam, with his head bowed hiding his smile said, Dee, Dee, tat a .'Falcon and Roma looked at each other "is that some kind of joke?" she asked.

"No," Sam said, "when I was just learning to talk really before I could pronounce words, after mother or dad would say the prayer I 'd always say that. Our God is listening and he knows what I said and meant. "

Roma sat. "And you people call us weird she buttered a piece of toast nibbled at it then said, "have either of you given anymore thought to what we discussed last evening?"

"The answer is no, Roma," Nadia said and she was conscious of Sam looking at her through eyes of love and repeat.

" Nadia," Falcon said "have you considered this; how do you know you will be accepted into his flock his hand of protection? Think about it. You have not been properly baptized you do not know the bible and nothing of his teachings, aren't you taking a chance my dear?"

"yes,' she surprised him with her reply, and "I've given that a great deal of thought but our answer is still no. I 'vet been reading Sam's bible and it says: God so loved the World that he gave his only begotten Son, that whosoever believeth in him should not perish but have everlasting life . Now,,,, I don't know really how that can be interpreted, but I read it to mean that if a person believes in Jesus and the Father and tries real hard to do what is right to be a good person, well everything 's going to be all right. I can be wrong I hope not," Sam gently squeeze her fingers in support.

"How touching,' Roma said, dryly observing the gesture of love.

" Shut up darling," Falcon told her and this time she heard a distinct note, of warning in his voice, she closed her mouth. Falcon said," Is there no, way we may reach a compromise?"

"No," Sam said, flatly rejecting the offer.

"He's just like his father," Roma blurted, " hard headed as a goat."

" and very proud to be" Sam said, smiling.

Roma nodded the extent to which she had agreed with Sam was impossible to tell from the curt gesture. Falcon's eyes were hard as he looked at Nadia. "My dear, you may make this enjoyable , or very unpleasant when time comes. I suggest you think about it." Falcon's , smile was evil. He pointed to his crotch. "You and I dear" she shook her head slowly.

"The same applies to Sam," Roma said.

""Sorry the young man told her I think I'll pass." He had no way of knowing his mother had spoken those same words to Roma more than twenty years ago, referring to Tom's offer.

"Allot of your mother in you too, darling." Roma said with a nasty grin and your mother is going to have allot in her before all this is over. "Do pardon the slight punch won't you?" Sam, shot visual daggers of hate, at the witch.

."Do either of you realize," Falcon said, "how hopelessly outnumbered you are ? how puny your powers are compared with ours? And how foolish you are to reject this offer of compromise?" Sam and Nadia merely looked at him, saying nothing "we really are not obligated to abide by any rules." Falcon confided in them. "Believe that . The only reason we are here is to give you young people a chance to come to your senses."

" He is not lying," the heavy voice said as it sprang into Sam's head, "you can accept the offer from the Devil's agent and become one of the undead. There will be no more trails and tests should that be your decision the choice is yours. Tested by both God and Satan?" Sam flung the silent question How much is to be place on my shoulders, and when does it end?" But the mysterious voice was silent. Both Roma and Falcon were once again aware of the strange power in the room, neither of them understanding it, " your decision, young man?" Falcon urged.

"Go to Hell!" Sam told him, both Roma, and Falcon laughed, Falcon saying , "oh we've been there many times. Even at it's best it is a dismal place. Then we'll do our best to avoid it " Sam locked eyes with Falcon,

"Very well" Roma said. "I would suggest the both of you enjoy your day of rest both she and the warlock vanished before their eyes, leaving behind them a foul odor of sulfur. Nadia's hand covered Sam's hand with hers and the gently squeezed it. "It'll be all right," he said a different odor covered the departing smell of Roma and Falcon. This one was hideous, stinking of stale blood and rotting flesh, of the grave and beyond. Nadia looked up, her nose wrinkling at the smell . Her, eyes widened face paling she began to scream. Sam started to turn around to see what Nadia was viewing something savage smashed into his head and he fell, tumbling into painful darkness.

" They have all withdrawn period," Bart, said he put his shotgun on the table, Betty frowning as the front sight scarred the polished wood. But she said nothing to her husband of so many years. Good years all of them wit no regrets. And she was sorry, she had called him a klutz so many times over the years, but even with that feeling of love and penitence, she had to smile . Bart was clumsy always had been she said prayers even when he tried such a simple task as changing a light bulb especially if he had to stand on a stepladder. For if he didn't fall off the ladder he would to drop one of the bulbs; usually the good one, but she loved him, with all her heart he was such a good and honest, decent, and god-fearing man.

Wayne, was saying to Bart that something has changed, "I may feel it, something drastic has happened you wait, you'll see, Alex will tell you that I 'm right."

" He is right, "Balloon's voice jarred them all. They still could not accustom themselves to Balloon's sudden appearance. Balloon said; "they will not be here. Ever. They will come for Jane on the day after tomorrow, their final day on earth."

" And, us?" Bart asked hopefully. " One could always keep a bit of optimism that the man might change his mind. We will exists this life together.."

"Jane," Betty, asked. " She is well,"

" that's not what I meant I know she has an ordeal ahead of her a terrible one. But she will endure it."

" You May's know that for sure, Alex,"

Betty said" I know." Then the voice faded and the house went still .

Chapter Eighteen

Sam's head was throbbing, with pain. The side of his head was sticky. He put his fingertips to his head and gingerly touched the aching. His fingers came away sticky groaning he attempted to sit up in darkness, he made it on the second attempt rested for a moment then got slowly to his feet swaying in darkness he looked around, he couldn't remember where he was at. As his eyes began to penetrate the room around him, he could tell he was in a large room, a damp basement he concluded. He was a little confused. Roma had assured them no physical action would be taken until that Friday evening. And of course you believed her. " you fool The words from the Devil's Whore?" How typically mortal." Sam's temper really got the best of him.

" Sermons I don't need."

" If you knew , she wasn't to be trusted why didn't you tell me?" you are your father's son all right."

"Where is Nadia?"

"it seems, I hear her screaming somewhere from a distance. Never take anything for granted," the voice said. "what!"

"Do not trust them further. But bare this in mind, remember your father's words at the airport I cannot guarantee she will not be hurt. If anything it was blessed by the Dark One! Now go to her." The speaker of mighty words and the producer of thunder appeared in the circle of stones, behind the mansion and once more sat on a bounder. He folded his massive arms across his chest. The manlike traveler appeared to waiting for someone. It was not a long wait. "Why didn't you tell the young woman saw the face of the Hooded One?"

"I think he is to be tested further but perhaps I should have is that what you wish me to do?"

"A test?

"A painful wicked one, warrior."

"What I want you to do ? I didn't want you here to begin with'.

" But I am here ."

"Obviously and instead of listening to the pleas of mortals and attempting to keep shaky fingers off buttons that would ruin the earth. I am with you wondering why my most powerful ally is sitting on a rock in a circle of stones erected to worship Satan.

"The foul one does not know of my presence."

"He suspects."

"Am I supposed to tremble with fear at that knowledge?" The Heavens rumbled with laughter.

"Hardly, but at the risk of being redundant this is not your place I should order you away .

"If you do, I shall obey'"

"yes, the most powerful voice in all the thousands of worlds seemed to sign. But have I ever?"

"No." And so I shall not this time." And with a rush of wind the voice faded, leaving the mightiest of God's Warriors sitting on the rock, thoughtfully stroking his beard..

As, Sam was searching the mansion for Nadia, he thought he heard organ music from a distance he debated several moments before deciding to take his 45. Pistol, then shook his head and left the weapon it was. Then it struck him that somebody had died , who had died he said more to himself all at once panic hit him hard, then he remember his father's words: I cannot guarantee she will not be hurt. as he listened to the unmistakable sounds of funeral music, the, it was becoming louder as he approached the room where the music was coming from he asked Falcon and Roma who had died and then the panicked hit him, so hard as if someone had pull a plug from his heart out!" Nadia!" He whispered, Nadia! He flung open the door he came to with each room yielding the same nothing he stopped In the center of the dimly lighted hall, staring at the open yawing door at the end of the hall. Flickering candlelight danced deceptively from the room, and a heady not unpleasant India essence drifted from the gloom. The music became louder, but this time it was accomplished by sounds of soft weeping from a amount of people. Sam walked toward the open double doors, the sound of footsteps. He stopped just inside the door, , just as the gloom and the music and the sweet odor of musk and jasmine enveloped him. He cut his eyes to the candlelit scene at the ends of the long narrow room a coffin lid open rested on the bier on deep black velvet. The body that lay within the beautiful corpse or who, it was Nadia. Sam's fragile world spun madly for a few seconds almost dropping him to the carpet. He maintained control rubbing his face with shaky hands, he took several steps closer to the coffin hoping all this was some kind of joke it was not Nadia was dead.

Chapter Nineteen

Roma and Falcon came to his side he looked at them closely; their faces were pale and drawn with real worry lines creasing their brows. Sam touched Nadia's hand cold and dread he withdrew his fingers "we are sorry" Falcon, said his voice deep and sepulchral

"Yes," Roma echoed his sentiments "even though we are worlds apart in worshiping masters she was my daughter from my womb, and I loved her in my own way."

"How......? Sam started to ask.

"Time enough for that, Falcon verbally restrained him, "but suffice to say we had nothing to do with Nadia's untimely demise and we both beg you to believe that."

"But you were going to kill us both!" Sam protested, once more touching Nadia's cold flesh. He shuddered " I want to know how it happened."

They gently led him from the scene of tragic young death at so young of age, I know that we made threats against you but my God, how may you think I would harm my own daughter across the room on both sides the chairs were filled with coven members but they did not at all resemble the men and women he had seen earlier, you looked exhausted, Sam, Falcon and Roma put her arms on his shoulders "let me get you some coffee or something to eat, and you may tell us where you have been for the last four hours."

"You don't know?" Sam asked..

"No" her reply was open and honest. Sam searched her face for some kind of signed that she was lying but there was none.

"No we did not killed her, but our master did."

"Satan?" That pig!" Roma spat the word with such venomous hatred Sam was stunned as she was clearing her mouth of something nasty.

"But he is your God, your master,"

Falcon injected "that is something we both want to speak to you about but first he signed I must go offer my apologies to Nadia whether she may hear me or not it is something I must do." He walked to the casket and gazed down at the face of death. There were tears rolling down his cheeks. Genuine tears.

"I don't understand." Sam said.

"is it too late for us?" Roma asked all the while gently leading the young man from the room off the large mourning room, there she sat him on the couch and shut the door behind her blocking out all sounds of the weeping the sad melodious notes of the organ, the soft scent of incense remained . All that Roma asked all the while gently leading him to the couch. Roma flung her arms toward the door and the scene behind. "It has come home to us Sam. Reluctantly at first ,I have to confess it but finally with more conviction than I have hundreds of years, I began to admire your God." Sam stood

"This is a trick." He turned to leave the room the sounds of Roma's weeping stopped him he turned real tears were streaming from her eyes "oh Sam, I 'm so confused I don't know what to do, where to turn none of us do. Do you think we would be able a person weeping and mourning if we didn't feel a terrible loss, and quilt about what happen to Nadia. We have spoken of nothing else for hours. Repentance the cold bloodedness of the creature we worshiped, yes even admired for centuries we want." she signed Sam returned to his seat on the couch besides Roma "I don't know what I may do. Nadia said you took her in the arms of God, May's you do the same thing for me Sam? Baptize if that is what it takes."

"Yes, you would have to renounce all other Gods, and you would have to be sincere in that renunciation, for my God may see into your heart."

"I know." she said softly "and for Falcon and myself, and a few of the others it would mean instant death? Yes, Sam the instant the holy water touches the flesh of the witch, warlock or the undead we die."

"You're willing to go that far?"

"Yes." The softly spoken one-word condemnation touched him as might a velvet encased hand gripping his heart he cut his eyes to the door.

"You've discussed this with all the people out there?"

"Every one of them,"

Sam leaned back on the couch closing his eyes this is just too much too much in one day. Test her, the thought came to him, but bit was his thought and not spoken from any outside source. He rose from the couch, " I'll be back in ten minutes, who wants to be baptized first?"

Her smile was warm and sincere to any one in that room. "As you wish Sam." He went to his room and filled a small bottle with blessed water from the church in Montreal, a member of the coven sat besides Roma. When Sam returned to the room one of the members from New York. He smiled at Sam I don't know all the right words he pulled out the holy water and touched the man's forehead. The man recorded backward in pain his flesh bobbing as the blessed liquid ate into his face the man began a sense of regression as his body plow back in time horrid stench filled the room. Soon there was nothing but a pile of rotting rags on the floor in front of the sofa Sam stood, stunned by it all Roma gently led him across the room to another couch this is going to be a terrible ordeal for you. I think you had better have a strong drink before you continue yes, he said you're right. He must have dozed off for a moment for when he open his eyes Roma was besides him, " it is time now Sam, don't think this is a dream it is not!"

"Now we will tell the real truth about your God! Shall we." As he listened to Roma speak her words, tearing at him as he suspected.

" let me tell you a story Sam, Satan broke all the rules coming here, speaking to us, he told us he would no longer abide by any rules of the game."

"The game?" Sam questioned

"Yes, Sam the game, a game among the two mightiest players in the universe and all others. A very profane one. The Foul One returned, appearing behind you. He is seldom seen in his natural form even by us. He is grotesque, hideous if you can."

"His presence often kills, should human eyes fall on his ugliness. Nadia's Did."

Sam touched the side of his head "who hit me?"

"The Dark One. He is everywhere at once as is your God, my God, I hope Sam?" She leaned forward until her face was only a few inches from his. "Will you teach me how to pray to your God before you baptize me?"

" If you would like that, for sure."

"oh, yes. I would like that more than anything in this world, for I know my time remaining is very short, and growing shorter."

"My God might….."

"No, "she shushed him, placing a soft finger to his lips "I know things you do not, now finish eating your sandwich, do you think Nadia would want me to be happy?"

"Is Satan still here?"

"He is everywhere that is not what I meant."

"I know yes, I may feel his presence, he is furious but unable to do anything about it.-His anger t is merely by my speaking with you, about your God. " Well, that puts the Dark One in a very badly position now. He May's make any moves against you." As she was sliding against him on the chair, the perfume she wore was a scent Sam had never smelled before: very pleasant not too heady not too light and as it assailed his nostrils, the essence seemed to relax him, wrapping him in a fragrant invisible arms, "you're very tired Sam," he heard her say, he nodded his head in agreement as fatigue hit him hard, why don't you sleep for awhile Sam, the rest will work itself out later"

He could vaguely remember soft music and scented candles and incenses everything was blocked from his mind, what does it matter? He thought as arms of incredible sweetness and softness slipped around him, cradling him gently.

" here Sam," Roma whispered between the rustling of clothing the soft snick of a clasp opening, " rest your head here!" she pulled his head to her breasts. Sam thoughts wondered, I knew they would be bear and beautiful. He opened his eyes no more than a slit, and found the breasts to be more than beautiful, the nipples were stiff and erect, and it seemed only natural his lips would find the papilla encircling. Sam, felt feverish, not the unnatural heat of sickness, but that is clothing was an encumbrance he did not need.

"Here," she said "let me help you," her fingers worked at the buttons of his shirt and Sam quickly felt the coolness of air on his bear arms. Pillowing his head against her breasts he could not think of one single reason why he should object as she worked at his belt buckle loosening the snap at his waistband. The stick of the zipped followed and he moved his legs assisting her in the lowering of his jeans. "Why is it wrong?" he asked

"it isn't wrong" she said.

"Yes, he said, " it isn't." Sam was conscious of cool air on his groin but he felt it wasn't worth the efforts to open his eyes and look, then he realized his underwear shorts had been removed. . Everything seems natural what could be more natural than a man, and a woman together he moved his head to the satiny smoothness of her naked belly and kissed the indentation of navel, aware of her womanly scent, as she moved her hand, fingers encircling his growing thickness stroking him into surging hardness bringing him through the manipulation of her skillful touch almost to the point of ejaculation. Then with one swift move, she mounted him laughing as she did so. A moment later, everything returned to Sam coming in such a rush it almost overwhelmed him with its magnitude. His father's warning, the warnings of the mysterious voice. "Nadia!" her memory leaped into his brain; what had happened, he recalled the vision he had shared with Nadia the scene of his father fighting the witch, this woman who had impaled herself on his maleness driving her way Frantically towards completion he began fighting the witch attempting to dislodge her from his e the same as his father tried to do those many years ago. Sam was very close to exploding his semen into her wetness she held hand to her waist with no more effort than if she were pinning a helpless baby to its crib and despite himself Sam, felt his juices boiling. They began to spill over, and then exploded using her inner muscles, Roma milked the last drop of precious semen from him pulled away from him and padded naked to a table. There, she picked up a vial of dark red blood opened the small bottle, and drained it into her. Sam was too weak to move as she began speaking in a language he did not understand the incantation evil as it rolled from her tongue. Lighting licked around the mansion, as thunder ripped the countryside, the smell of burning sulfur strong in the stormy air. Laughter reached Sam's ears spilling from the other room. Hot, wild rage filled him causing his blood to run strong giving him the strength to claw on his clothing and stagger from the room where he had been seduced into an unwilling par amour. The scene that greeted him was of the vilest imaginable a grotesque real-life panorama, more vivid than anything Hollywood could ever produce in its most brutish moods. Nadia, had been lifted from the casket, pillows placed under her she was naked, her lifeless body propped up on pillows her legs spread apart knees to feet hung out of the casket. Falcon was among her thighs his maleness erect, pumping in and out of the young woman shouting his rage, Sam charged the sickness before he was kicked and beaten into semi-consciousness. He lay bloodied on the carpet, unable to stop the hideousness taking place. Falcon's hardness became slick with blood, and Sam could not understand that for Nadia was dead. Then he decided in his near delirium, it was not blood merely the way the candles cast their dubious flickering light. Nadia's head was thrown back, her mouth a black gaping hole, eyes closed in surrender on her voyage to the stygian shore Falcon continued to ram his maleness into her.

"Why don't you pray, mother fucker?" a female voice screeched at Sam. He looked up through his pain into wild eyes of Lana, squatting half naked besides him, Sam shook his head as the taunts began profane and loud, exhorting him to call on his God for help. He fought to get to his feet, but hands turned into fists pounding him into the carpet he watched as the ugly act of Necrophilia drew closer to completion, Falcon lunging in Ernesto burying his long thickness into the dead flesh of Nadia. The man howled like an animal as he ejaculated, spilling into the young woman. Falcon, arrogantly rose from the satin-lined casket like some monster from the grave and stepped onto the floor wiping his softening penis with a towel handed him from one of those as lost as he, Sam lay his head on the carpet and wept.

"Oh, don't be such a cry baby Sam,!" Roma's voice cut at him "you may have her back now." She raised her hand performed a ritual that was too quick for Sam to follow. He shifted his eyes to the sounds of someone suddenly weeping and thought he was going utterly mad as Nadia's eyes opened and she looked around her, a bewildered expression on her face as if she not only did not understand where she was but why she was crying she looked down at her nakedness then at her temporary home, and screaming joined the tears. Roma laughed "there is your darling, Sam. Take her and witnessed what marvelous parturient pops from her womb. You won't have a long wait for when my master takes a hand in events such as the one now growing within Nadia's womb develop rapidly, such wonders to perform. Take your darling, Sam and both of you carry your sniveling selves from this room. So we lost a member from your application of holy water." She answered the puzzled looked in his eyes "no great loss it is an honor to die for the master's he cackled like the witch that she was.

Chapter Twenty

"How does it feel to be beaten, young man and woman of God? The room of lost and damned should howl with laughter." Sam pulled himself to his knees and wiped blood from cuts above his eyes. When he turned to look at the witch, she hissed with fright and drew back from the sight of his burning eyes. "We're not beaten you whore. I 'm whipped for now, but I 'm not down for the count. I don't understand what has taken place here for I know Nadia was dead, no one could look that dead and not be dead. I don't know if I'll ever understands what has taken place here but I know this for some reason you May's or won't kill us .....Yeah" he said slowly his eyes shifting to Nadia, "she got to be kept alive right? Sure. I see that."

"Me I don't know but I 'm going to beat you Bitch." His eyes lashed at the witch. Someway, somehow, I 'all win this battle, bet on it." Sam rose to his feet and walked to the candle lighted brier helping Nadia to the floor. No one tried to stop him no one attempted to interfere he ripped a drape from one of the windows to cover Nadia up with they walked from the room between the jeering,, ugly sounds of the unbelievers.

"Sam?" Nadia spoke in a whisper even though the room and all the evil of its occupants was farther behind them with each step. "I was dead!"

"I know, honey and don't ask me to explain it, cause I May's?"

"Sam?"

He looked at her taking, her offered hand, "I know what you have to do." They were on the second floor of the great house, walking down the corridor to their rooms, "what Nadia?"

"You have to make love to me as quickly as possible."

"I don't understand."

"Yes. You do, the voice boomed in his head. And, can your seed be very strong."

" I heard the voice that time Sam," she told him "and that's why you have to make love to me"

"You remember Falcon raping you?"

"Every, awful ugly second of it. I May's explain it, for I couldn't move, not even my eyes. But I could feel the pain. It's, I know I was dead Sam, but I wasn't I know my heart Stopped when I looked up and saw that thing, what in God's name was that?"

"I didn't see it, but Roma said it was the Devil. I guess that much of what she said was true your heart stopped?"

"Yes. I came back when Falcon......began raping me something else."

"Sam."

" What?"

"I saw you and Roma."

"But you were."

" I know but I could still see you. Both. I was so proud of you when you fought through the drug and began to resist."

" The food was drugged:?

"No the perfume she was wearing, was an ancient aphrodisiac, she stayed within the rules of the game in the world while we're here ."

" Sam , we're not of this world we're kind of in limbo," Sam was conscious of that mighty presence near, "you go take a shower, Sam . You smell like well like her. I 'vet go to do something maybe it will help."

" what?" Sam asked innocently. She looked at him and shook her head.

"Douche." she said

Sam tended to his face after the shower, applying antiseptic to small cuts one eye was puffy, the area under it turning a shade of greenish blue, and there were numerous smaller bruises on his face and chest and legs. But he concluded he would live. How long and what for is the question, he muttered.

"How skeptical you are." The voice spoke to him. "Weren't you warned you would be tested? And wasn't it I who told you not to fear should you sometimes fail?"

"I'll did a pretty good job of failing this night didn't I ?" Sam said glumly.

"so did your father, but he found a place besides God.."

" Am I right in doing what I 'm we're about to do?"

" I cannot answer that. That is something only you and the young woman may decide."

" What if Falcon's seed takes hold? She would birth something truly awesome and terrible."

"Your seed with Roma was strong, and she will please her dark Master.'"

"So I have to try to overcome Falcon's seed?"

" I told you I cannot answer that for you."

" Why do I feel that I 'm about to do is right, but with a nagging feeling of guilt that is somehow wrong ?" But the mighty force had gone. Sam feeling the invisible presence fade from his brain. He looked up as Nadia entered the room, " you said we'd know his reasons for throwing us together like this, Sam. And it wouldn't be a mortal question or issue we are facing, the real reason; doing what is right?"

" I think so, Nadia."

she smiled "I hate to quote an old line, Sam, but please be gentle with me I hurt all over." He was very gentle with her. Their loving making was pure, somehow sanctified and when it was over they slept, lost in exhaustion.

Something entered the room, something awesome in its righteous power, and it guarded the two as they slept. "Sam?" she whispered, her mouth close too his ear.

" Umm?"

"I want us to get married."

It took a moment for that to register with him, he finally cocked his head on the pillow and blinked rapidly several times.

"Say again!"

"You heard me." She lifted herself up on one elbow and stared down at him. Thick strands of long silken hair shading on one side of her face.

"Nadia I mean how? Who would perform the ceremony? I really doubt we could leave this house or at least the immediate grounds."

"We'd have to leave." she shushed him with a soft kiss, they have JPs in your country that marry people, and judges they aren't ministers, so what makes them any better than you ?"

" Me!" This is weird Nadia, and certainly illegal."

" I 'm not concerned with mortal law, Sam and I 'm really not sure it would be acceptable in the eyes of God."

"Probably not, I just want the words from you and from me, from out of our hearts, so let's get cleaned up get dressed and go into the timber and get married now!"

Sam knew with only the knowledge reasonably intelligent men possess concerning their limited understanding of women, that it would be best not to argue just get up and follow her orders.

"He is pleased," Roma spoke to Falcon over coffee in her quarters "our Master said he was most happy with the way matters are preceding.

"Are you with child?"

"Yes. I may feel the demon growing in me."

"When will you give birth?"

"On the sixth day of the sixth week precisely on the sixth hour."

"How prophetic. The mark of the beast (666) and your chances my dear."

"None I will die for the master, the demon will live forever. As Tom was meant too. . But I failed there, I am admittedly u un-knowledgeable on such matters, they occur so rarely,"

"How is forever possible?"

"A demon have you ever seen one, Falcon?"

He shook his head, "not on earth."

"They are of and for the Devil, projected by him; only a holy child born in the same time frame from the same father may kill the master's son. And since you battered Nadia's cunt so well. The odds of that happening are infinitesimally minute."

"The same time frame?" Falcon looked confused.

"(666) day, week, month and minute."

" But not necessary at precisely the same moment as your birthing."

"That is correct."

Falcon was thoughtful for a few seconds, " it is reasonable to assume Balloon's boy-child of love coupled with Nadia last night?"

" I would think so. But your seed is much more powerful, Falcon, older with strength of the master. No I think she is a demon child."

Falcon was not so certain but he hid his doubts, and changed the subject.

"There was an intruder in the house last night. I am very much surprised you did not sense the presence an. Intruder, Falcon ?"

The warlock's only reply was to lift his eyes upward, "You are certain?"

" As certain as I know Nadia's cunt was tight." The monster took no umbrage to her statement, " male or female? "

" Male warrior." The witch and the warlock looked at each other, gazes all knowing, holding.

"So he had shipped out again." It was not a question from Roma.

"It's been many years since that one took any direct action on earth." Falcon said "Joan de Arc,

"That we know of," Roma corrected him "I don't like this. That one had bested our master on more than one occasion."

" Don't let him hear you say that you know how our Prince hates the Warrior."

" There may be no mistake this time Falcon, I must get Nadia and leave this place. The demons must be birthed; we May's take a chance on staying." Falcon's face showed his concern and something else.

Roma read the silent worry lines," what Falcon?"

" My dear I don't believe we may leave until it is concluded. The Master might make an exception for you, n your condition, but the rest of us…" He left it at that.

"What are you babbling about?

He shook his handsome head, "not babble, Roma I spoke with the Dark One's emission early this morning just before dawn. She told me that Wheatfield is cut off; no escape, all is lost except for the taking of Balloon's whore."

" Is that why our Master returned here?, angry, brooding."

"But I spoke with him last night he is not angry with us he knows the warrior is here or at least suspects it, and is furious that his enemy would allow such a breech of the rules."

Roma laughed, "those so-called rules are unimportant mostly a myth."

"But our Master believes his enemy should abide by those rules, since he professes to be so holy." Roma quietly picked up on the reversal of roles among herself and Falcon. "You have suddenly become quiet Knowledgeable, darling."

" Your time is short, Roma and growing shorter with each tick of the clock. He has elevated me to a more lofty position here on earth."

" Congratulations, Falcon; it was only a matter of time." He nodded his acceptance and appreciation of her felicitation. "He is mulling over a suggestion of mine."

. "Oh?"

" That we breech all rules of the game kill the young warrior now, just after we call out the forces present invisibly at all black masses."

"Well I think It's dangerous, Falcon and Could easily get out of control, have you ever seen the calling out of the forces?"

" Truthfully no but Tom once told me in Germany, three centuries ago back when I was a young buck that he witnessed it once, said it was quiet spectacular in a bell-book-an-candle. He was quiet young when he saw it done, I believe he said it came very close to frightening him."

"It is frightening Falcon. And in my condition I could not witnessed it, too dangerous." She was thoughtful for a moment, "while it is dangerous calling out the spirits you must have done some research on the subject."

Falcon smiled.

"I thought as much." She, returned the devilish smile." if God's warrior is here, t that would infuriate the ancient warrior, and he would fight, for it , for it is his nature to do that, our forces might win and I stress might, but if they lost, it would seriously deplete our odd forces on earth."

" I took that into consideration, we would call out only those within a certain prescribed distance of this locale, and only every other one, thereby insuring us a reserve wise."

"When did our master say he would reach his decision?"

"An hour before dawn, tomorrow if our master's reply is yes, a special mass will be called for tomorrow night, midnight. You will need two virgins and another young one for the alter to cut out her heart."

" We have them the children from the city, Tom will have to take part and that is the only stumbling bloc that I see."

She shook her head. "My son is weak, and not to be trusted, but I think perhaps a visit from the dark one might put some steel in his backbone."

Falcon arched an eyebrow expressively

"I will speak to the Prince."

Falcon nodded and turned to leave "Oh," he said "I saw Nadia and God's young warrior leaving the house a moment before I came up here, they were Practically beaming with love I found it disgusting for a moment.,

Roma was flung back in time to Wheatfield and Fork county, to the little creek besides which two lovers lay , performing a marriage ceremony without benefit of a legal entanglements she smiled a bittersweet movement. the smile touched with evil.

" Why are you smiling?" Falcon asked

" I was thinking about a marriage I witnessed back in "56" in Wheatfield, yes. I think Sam and Nadia are about to do the same."

"It must have touched you Roma for you to remember something so trivial after all these years."

Her returning gaze was hard, "In a manner of speaking I puked after them

left."

Chapter Twenty One

"Here." Nadia said looking at the familiar surroundings. "Where you made me a Christian.

"I just dropped a few sprinkles of water on your head."

" Why are you smiling Sam?" He pulled out a tiny vial of water I think we may spare this don't you?"

Sudden tears sprang in her eyes, "oh, Sam I love you."

"I love you too." He gently kissed her mouth. "You got the bible?" He did not notice the tiny marks on the side of her neck, right above the vein.

"Did you hear that I sensed his presence in the room this morning. Strong and male and fearless. I was going to say something strong and male and fearless."

"The hooded one has made his decision young warrior. You young warrior are marked for death, a special black mass has been called for tomorrow night. They will attempt to call out the forces of darkness, if they succeed I will do battle with them."

" You will know at midnight tomorrow night if their calling had been successful. If so, you must take your wife and leave the house immediately. Do not attempt to fight them alone they are too wily for your young age. You both must run and hide in the timber. But a word of warning you cannot travel past the set of boundaries you will know them for they are easily to be seen. Remember young warrior your sole purpose is to destroy this coven and the tablet if possible."

"Tablet? What tablet? Sam asked.

"The Devil's Tablet, it is here hidden.

"And if I destroy it, what happens?"

"That is an unanswerable question, for it has never been destroyed."

"Wonderful." Sam said sarcastically, "how will I know this tablet?"

"It will know you, the table t is evil, and you represent good."

While Sam cleaned, and oiled his weapons and set up their backpacks with food and supplies Nadia went down to the kitchen for food, to last them for the coming days ahead. She felt like a stranger in her own home. "We are alone except for Linda,"

"There is something about Linda I can't put my fingers on it."

"What is the story on her?" What is among Linda, and you? She shook her head I hope I 'm wrong about her?"

"Sam, I 'm not jealous, we used to share a room."

"Tom had a few dates with her in school, my brother told me that she didn't put out that's why he stopped dating her. But he told me enough about you to get her interested, and she talked about you almost nonstop almost as if she were desperate to get with you. I had to get out, move into a different room but that's not the main reason ,

"Sam. I don't trust her. I think she's one of them." She averted her eyes to the door. "And they don't know it."

"I don't follow you honey."

"All right then, there a peculiar mark on Linda's chest just under her left breast."

"She saw me looking at it and told me it was a birthmark. Sam I've seen others like it, on people visiting here at Falcon house. One time that same mark was on all the people here."

"What does the mark look like?"

"A five pointed star."

"Pentagram."

"I know from watching horror movies that has something to do with black magic, the occult."

"Why didn't you tell me before this Nadia?"

"I never gave it much thought Sam, things were happening so fast around Here it just slipped my mind. Then all of the sudden the other day, when she was sitting with us at the table, it came to me like a sixth sense in my head." She sighed, "maybe I 'm paranoid and maybe not,"

Sam said thoughtfully "we'll just have to play it by ear while we're getting ready to run."

She came to him and put her arms around his waist, "hold me Sam." She was trembling and Sam could sense it, with the recently acquired powers of perception and silent communication, which the trembling had nothing to do with fear.

"What's the matter honey?"

"I know something is wrong, but I May's read your mind don't ask me how I know Sam, I…I've read and heard that some women just sense when they're pregnant and I 'm pregnant I know it ." Sam thought forgetting that she could read his thoughts I wonder if the baby belongs to me or Falcon.

"That's the problem Sam, I don't know."

" You are to remain close to Sam." The burning voice scorched into the brain of the receiver, " if all fails here and he dies then your only mission in life will be to stay with Nadia and make certain of the well being of the child growing in her womb. Accept whatever comes your way, be it feigned faith in their God, or the life of poverty or prostitution only the child's welfare is important do you understand?"

"Yes. Master," her voice was full of strength and awe.

"You are a good actress. Your show to date has been superb I compliment you."

"Thank you Master it was all for you."

"Don't become pushy, Bitch! I cannot tolerate such behavior you are a woman , your purpose in life is to fuck, receiving, maleness in whatever hole they choose to stick it in, don't forget what I told you."

" I shall not, Master."

"For your sake I hope not now go to them.

Chapter Twenty Two

"Sam!" Nadia looked at Sam, "your sweetie, darling," she said, her voice as warning as an aortic breeze in the dead of winter. "Retract claws dear Sam, we don't know anything for sure."

" I know one thing make those two things."

"And that is? "

"She's got the hoot's for you, and if she tries to come on to you I'll scratch her bald head." Sam nodded his head as he moved toward the door. Remembering Nadia's was right cross in the den. He opened the door cautiously, tensely, expecting anything to come leaping at him but Linda stood there looking pale and frightened and really, Sam thought real pretty.

"I read that." Nadia projected.

"Damn!"

"Come in Linda," he closed the door behind

"Wow she said what happened to your face?"

"Little accident," Sam said, not really lying to her. "I'll tell you about it later. I uh-just wanted to be with you guys for a few minutes, that's all maybe have dinner with you all this evening if that's okay?"

"Of course, Nadia answered for the both of them," thinking where would you like to start eating, eating on Sam?

"And I read that honey, you're going to read allot more before this evening is over"

"You guys went off somewhere this morning." Linda said "I got a little panicky."

Nadia was hammering mental thrusts at Linda attempting to enter her mind she could not. Her attitude softened a bit toward the young woman as she detected truth in her statement still there was something about her.... Some little vagueness Nadia could not pinpoint.

"We went for a walk in the timber." Sam said. "And got married, Nadia thought so hands off, babe and she mentally tallied up the events of the past twenty=four hours. Where were you when I was getting raped by Falcon's baseband bat it's not that big Sam, projected it wasn't sticking in you dear true thank God. Linda said I don't know what's been the matter with me lately I sleep so soundly even when I lie down just to nap. I've never done that before sleep so much I mean. It's the cold clean air, Sam suggest Linda solemnanly shook her head No. Sam it's much more than that. And I think you two know it is. I 'd like to leave go back to Carrington would one of you take me?" Sam signed, cutting his eyes to Nadia she shrugged sit down Linda, he said I guess we'd better talk.

Jane stood at her window, gazing out at the quiet street. It was ominously silent in Wheatfield for a time, there had been faint sounds of hammering, they were preparing for her now it was silent. Jane looked down at her hands and was reminded of an old TV. Commercial, she used to have the hands of a twenty year old. The hammering was meant for her to hear it; they wanted her to hear it. She looked down at her hands again, soon they would be putting the nails through her hands, would it hurt she asked herself when they drive the nails through hands.

The mist that was Alex Balloon, hovered silently watching Jane, knowing every thought in her mind, but unable to help her, for what she was thinking was true. And if a being from the other side could sigh, Balloon did, knowing she would have to endure almost unbearable pain for a time before he could step in the end it. She would be humiliated, sexually assaulted tortured, tested only then could he end it. And after Balloon did that he would really end it, and Wheatfield would be no more.

Bart and Betty, Wayne, and Anita sat in the growing darkness of the living room discussing the bible they knew they should turn on some lights, but they did not want to break the feeling of closeness they were sharing. Just outside of the city, the beasts had gathered to feast on the bodies of Those who had died in Wheatfield. They snarled and growled and ripped the dead meat from the bones stuffing their fanged mouths as the drool dripped from their jaws, leaking in slimy ribbons to foul the ground. The males found human females amid the piles of bodies a female who, had pretended to be dead, who was suffering from only minor injuries. And as was their custom, they dragged her screaming to the oldest male amid them, the leader. Her shrieks as they tore the clothing, changed to wails of pure terror as the big male pushed her to her bear knees and mounted her under the cool moonlight of western fall. When the oldest male had finished, the other males according to age and ranks in the pecking order of things took their turn with the woman each biting her on the neck as they lunged deep within her. Her body would be covered, with thick coarse hair, her face would change. The jaw enlarging and she would be as them, she would be able only to mumble and snarl and growl, and the beasts would understand her, and she them. She would not remember any worshiping of the God she thought she was deceiving, as she prayed and lied . And she would be happy in her new form.

Chapter Twenty Three

"The pentagram on your chest."

"That's a birthmark, Nadia. I swear before God it is you've got to believe me. "Somewhere in the house, a wailing began containing a familiar note of pain and terror. "What in God's name is that?" Linda asked

"You've never heard it before? Sam asked "you don't know?"

"No Sam, I swear it."

"That's one of the young girls brought in kidnapped from god knows where. She is being raped from both ends probably passed around amid some pretty heavy hung guys. She's not enjoying it very much is she?"

Tears sprang into her eyes. "I don't want that done to me ever. Oh, God believe me, both of you, I 'm a Christian I go to church every Sunday I worship God, not the Devil. Please help me, believe me get the bible," the bible was placed next to Linda. Nadia released her hands Linda grabbed up the Holy book and clutched it to her, her tears dropping onto the leather of the book.

"As God is my witnessed." she said, " I love only him. I swear it." Holy water, on the young woman's forehead, nothing happened.

Nadia leaned back in her chair nodding her heard.

"Roma told me the holy water only works if, you're a witch, or warlock or the undead."

"What a performance!" The burning words seared into the girl's head you almost had me weeping over the dilemma, "but water and I don't mix very well such a pity it wasn't Oscar night, you would have won hand down."

"Thank you Master." And the evil force was gone from the room.

"You had better understand young man, your mother is too bare me a demon," the hot words penetrated Tom's brain, "she must be taken care of with the utmost of delicacy. Do you understand young man I will not tolerate any further backbiting from you. No more plotting against the female who birthed you. She soon will have served her purpose on earth and Will be called home to me."

"I understand, Master, Falcon"

"Oh, you are a schemer, aren't you? Not a drop of loyalty in you. Only to You Prince. Bah! Only to me because you are afraid of me, you shit your pants each time we communicate do you really believe young man, that you may beat your mentor?"

"Sir, Falcon is not my mentor he is an idiot."

" Perhaps he is that to a point, but he has loyalty and that is something you do not possess."

"What may I do to prove my love for you?"

"Obey orders for one thing." The voice had a tinge of dryness to it. Have patience young schemer for you are but a child in the order of darkness. You have this life to live before anything of any significance is to be placed into your greedy hands."

Tom was pout, " I should have been born a true demon."

"Yes. But you weren't and there is nothing even I may do about that."

"He has spoken." Falcon said. "We will tempt to call out the forces this evening."

Roma lay on her bed she did not feel well, because of the demon within her womb, and she was in a great deal of pain much of the time. "I wish you great deal of luck Falcon," she whispered "but I must add this note of warning, watch Tom, for his plotting now includes you. The master has warned him that I must be protected, but you have no such assurances from the Prince be careful."

"Then Tom is a fool! He under estimates me, Roma. I can be forced to kill him or have him killed."

"He should have died at birth." The mother said turning her head away, biting her lips as waves of pain struck her, cramping her. Falcon watched her twist on the sheets. "Is there nothing I may do?"

"Only tell me that Nadia is in the same agony."

"I am afraid she is not."

"That does not mean she is undergoing a normal gestation period. The sperm can be in combat within her. It could be days, even weeks before the matter is decided it is entirely possible it will not be decided. Until the moment of birth or even weeks afterwards. It depends on who is present if one of our kinds is there and has the power from the Prince it could even take month's years. I know of such cases in any event I will not know the outcome for sometime.

"Why, Roma?"

" Because I will be gone."

"Roma? He walked to the bed of the Devil-induced pain, "what of the demon?

"If it is a true demon, and believe I know that it is a true demon, it will need very little assistance after the birthing. Only a week or, so of suckling. Then the metamorphosis is so rapid it is not only unbelievable it is also utterly terrifying in its majesty."

" I Falcon struggle for words."

"Go Falcon you have much to do and I do not wish you to witness my suffering. Go." He moved away from the bed walking to the door he paused.

"I will tell you how things went this night Roma."

She laughed, and her laughter chilled him, "if you live through it.,"

Sam awakened the ladies roughly no gentleness' to his touch he spoke the same message to each woman: "Get up, and get dressed."

"What happened Sam? Nadia asked! Rubbing the sleep from her eyes.

"I think we're about to witnessed the most awesome event to ever occur on the face of this earth." He smiled, "other than that fellow who was born in Bethlehem, that is." He sobered again remembering what the Voices told him, the calling out of the forces of darkness? "It's going to happen tonight.

"He came to you? He told you?"

"No. I just know. Sam shook his head, "I don't know Nadia maybe he did come to me in a dream, I have no recall of any conversation among us. I just woke up and knew it was going to happen."

"I'm scared half out of my mind." Linda said,

"That's makes it a club of three." Sam replied. In the lush timber behind the house a shadowy figure drifted in and out of the tall trees. While his movement seemed vague and uncertain the tall warrior was actually deep in thought his musing troubled and sometimes dark with fury of all things that held sway outside of the firmament. The warrior hated Satan with a passion that border lined on disobedience to the teaching of God the father indeed the warrior had come close to admonition from him on more than one occasion for his passionate hatred of Satan. The warrior had pledged with him for Millennia to destroy the beast once and for all. Have done with the Filthy one. End it. Call his people home, but the master of all things would merely shake his great head and say not yet. And the warrior knew that not yet would apply to this blinking in the span of all things, as well he knew no fear of the demons and the other grotesque creatures that would soon be called to appear. He had destroyed their kind many times in the past and would this time not. What trouble the old warrior was, the mystery in the house of the evil one, and should be alert the young Christian offspring of Balloon to that mystery?"

No. he decided I may do only so much without overstepping the boundaries. Really he concluded I have probably interfered too much as it is. He stopped by the filthy sin-encrusted circle of the dark stone's and looked toward the house. No young warrior you must cope with the mystery by yourself. I will help in other matters but in this your strength must be all Powerful your faith all-believing and never wavering and your cunning at its zenith. God be with you.

"You are too close." The voice boom in his head, " It is dangerous where you are and it is not advisable for mortals to view this awfulness."

"I have to see what I am too fight." Sam replied as Nadia and Linda looked at him in surprises.

"Very well, have it your way young warrior." The mighty voice faded.

"What is that noise," Linda, asked.

" The beasts stirring on the ridge of the torch lit circle." The foil on top of the ridge watched as a shadowy figure moved closer to the light walking in a peculiar, hunkered manner. Even at this great distance they looked grotesque….. Not human. "The beasts, Nadia said.

"I wonder where they came from." Sam mused aloud, "I mean what is their origin?"

"Hell. I suppose,." She replied, "I don't know, Sam you know as much about them as I do."

Linda was strangely silent, "God's failure!" The phrase leaped into Sam's mind and the young man questioned that statement, "but how may.. Could God fail at anything?" He wished for the mighty voice, but it was silent. He remembers something his mother said, something that she said his real father had said, nobody knows how many times God tried to make man in his own imagine and failed. Sam pondered on that for a moment; thinking was the beasts God's failures? What happened to cause the failure?

Chapter Twenty Four

There's something going on down there." Linda said, "Look." The participant in the calling of the forces had gathered in circles several rings of them each growing progressively smaller inward, the beasts forming the larger outer circle. The circles began moving the first clockwise the inner circle counter clock wise. It was a grotesque form of dancing. The women dancing back to back the men front to front. They hummed lowly the faint humming only occasionally reaching the ridge. Standing by the dark alter was Falcon, his face whitened with make-up in stark contrast to his black robe. The humming changed into chanting, the dancing becoming more profane. The chanting turning into a low roar as three young girls were dragged screaming through the dancing leaping, chanting circles of worshipers, one was stripped naked, her clothing ripped from her body. She was secured to the alter, her legs spread wide, bent at the knees. She could not have been more than eleven or thirteen. "I don't want to watch this. Nadia said loud enough for Sam to hear her. Sam's face remained impassive. He said nothing he knew something was going on among Nadia and Linda.

"Call the hyenas!" A voice screamed and the chanting grew thunderous. 'Doges Doges,' the circle screamed. 'Hear out cries, O, Doges.' "Call the Centaur!" The voice commanded. A lamb was dragged into the circle. Its throat was cut and the blood sprinkled around the alter, encircling the naked, weeping girl. "Centaurs, Centaurs those who prances, for the Prince of Darkness. Ilion and Nehalem Centaurs and magnesia, come to us now. Call the satyrs,!"

"Doomsdays! Dion! Flesh eater and Lord of all that is pleasurable come join us." Now the flesh of the lamb was ripped from its body and passed about the circle of dancers, gnawing at the bloody strips of meat. 'Call the griffin!' The chant went up, 'call the owl and the Raven!' And Sam heard the beating of wings overhead. Something was close to his head. Instinctively, he Ducked, the talons just missing his head.

'Call the great kulich! Bring on the bats and the rats!' The forest surrounding them became eerily, silently then a faint scurrying sound was heard and something furry and evil brushed against Sam, Nadia muffed a screamed, Sam whirled the bat that was entangled in her hair. He finally slapped it free and the furry filth went flapping and screeching off into the night toward the torches and the stones. "Tom!" Falcon shouted. "Now!" He pointed to the terrified girl bound naked at the alter. Tom jumped upon the alter. Like Falcon he was dressed in black robes. He lifted his robe exposing his erect maleness lunging at the girl; he tore at her bloody body as he tore his way inside her, laughing at her pitiful screaming. Falcon ran to her his teeth shining brightly in the torchlight fanged he bent his head and tore at the vein in her neck, sucking her blood just as Tom, began his ejaculation. Falcon looked up at the girl's throat, blood leaking from his mouth he pointed to the sky as a horrible creature sluggishly made its way through the darkness. Others in the coven rushed up to get their share of the girl's gushing blood; a member of the coven took Tom's place among the girl's legs. Lunging at her as her body began to pale from the loss of blood. "I really don't believe I 'm seeing the things, looks like a half man half fish. Call the little people," Falcon shouted "come imps you have your master's permission come!"

Nadia asked Sam?" what is that smell?"

"Sulfur," Sam whispered.

"It's more than that," Nadia said, "it's evil."

Linda looked at her. The sky was now a color of hell, the flames real or imagined licked the area above them, dancing down out of he sky. The sky was suddenly filled with bats, hundreds of them, their excrement falling to the ground with soft ploys. The ground around the circle wriggled with rats, their red reflecting dully in the torch light and the strange coloration of the sky. "Hear me, O, Lord of Filth. Hear, my cries, O Prince of Darkness. Hold us close to Your chest. Apollo. Let us taste more of your foulness, touch us with your lips let us hear the sounds of your Cloven Hooves. For us, a soul is yours send the Serpents and the Demons the denied and the defiled, come to us little people!" And as if Merlin had suddenly waved his magic wand, the ground around the alter was filled with satanic imps, dancing and leaping and laughing wickedly. The wind picked up speed and strength and coldness over the land, blowing first cold then hot, confusing the elements Falcon's voice grew stronger ringing over the night-draped red-tinged, evil-enveloped the countryside. "Amadeus! Baliol Beelzebub! Mephistopheles! We who serve you implore you to rip away the veil and send all the forces to us. We are in need of the help only you may send; we stand in awe of your majestic power, Great one." Each push, brought wails of rains from the chills. The flickering flame from the torches seemed to join and mingle with bloody red of the sky. Sam then noticed the third she had brought her, moving no more than an inch or two each time. They had not noticed her all their attention riveted on the scent of rape and defilement, on the bloody alter.

"She's going to make a break for it." Sam muttered." I'll bet you that's Janet, I've got to help her."

"Sam…..!" Nadia protested.

"No it's something I have to do she's suffered enough."

The look in Linda's eyes was strange a mixture of loathing and respect.

"I 'm going down to that second ridge." Sam pointed checking the Thompson the full drum was fitted in the belly of the smog. The canvass pouch filled with chips on Sam's belt. He turned to look at Nadia. "I will be back," he said.

" I know." she said, then stood and watched him slowly make his way down the gently sloping hill until he was lost from view. The red darkness swallowing him. The circle of dancers pushed forward as Falcon began his climax, withdrew and stepped from the alter, wiping his bloody penis on The rag that was once the young's girl's shirt. Janet did not move with the crowd staying in place half hidden.

Chapter Twenty Five

Just outside the limit of the torchlight. A huge wooden cross was brought to the alter, driven upside down behind the dark and bloodied stone. The girl was jerked from the alter and dragged to the cross. Strong hands held her upside down as hammers and spikes began their gruesome work. Her screaming as she was crucified seemed to fill the small valley. She was left hanging upside down spikes in her hands and feet, to wail out what life was left in her. But it was not yet over for the girl. They would return to her one more time. "Send us the demons!" Falcon said, his voice carrying full and strong "send them, O, Great One." The sky became entirely red its bloody hues casting slick shadows over the grounds. The rats and the bats ceased their scurrying and flapping the imps were silent, and the only sound to be heard was the moaning of the girls behind the alter. Nailed to a cross. Janet slipped deeper into the shadows she looked toward the ridge where she had seen on a flash of light reflecting off metal. She moved toward the high ground moving slowly attracting no attention. Sam waited. Linda moved up silently behind Nadia her fist balled.

"Now!" Falcon screamed the one-word plea. "Now!" The growled circle one massed ring of evil echoed. The sky seemed to split wide open.. Great stinking clouds of evil-smelling settled over the house of the Devil. Janet edged deeper into the dark red of false night, moving faster now, her youth giving added strength to her legs. Great grotesque creatures filled the sky two headed amphisbaena were flung out of the gaseous mist reptilian basilisks coiled and hissed and rolled to earth winged clawed griffins snorting from the demon head the deformed and monstrous Su, with its feathered tail and horned head, suddenly appeared around the circle its mighty claws digging into the ground the gluon, a creature so hideous as to be indescribable howled as it came to earth from behind the hot curtain of hell the clawed, many-headed hydra came to rest on earth, its hideousness only slightly less than the great ruche that beat its way to earth, its feathered still smoking from the pits. The owls and the ravens and centaurs and satyrs and hyenas joined the now crowded circle all gathering around the cross where the girl hung in torment, spikes holding her upside down. The blood leaking from the wounds dripping into her eyes. "Tom!" Falcon called, "come it is time for the final act." The young man stepped forward a sadistic gleam in his eyes a sharp curved knife in his hands. The girl began wailing as the bald cut strips of flesh from her body, cutting tracing of vulgar images in her skin. Tom chanted as he worked with Falcon besides him, calling on all the dark forces of the Netherworld. The rite as old as this world was finally concluded. Then with no thought of mercy, Tom cut out the girl's heart and he and Falcon ate the still trembling muscles. The warrior was near, watching trembling with dark rage and hate swelling within him. But the mighty warrior from the firmament was powerless to interfere. He had to turn away from the bloody scene of sacrilege. For his eyes and thoughts could kill and as much as he wanted to do just that, it was not his place to so yet.

Janet lay besides Sam on the ridge overlooking the scene of outrage Sam had fought back the temptation to raise the Thompson and blow the Devil worshiper back to hell. But the range was far too great and beside, he knew it was not yet time, for that he would have to wait. "Come on he whispered to the girl let's go."

"Are we going to be all right?" Janet asked "I hurt from what they did to me you know?"

" I think we're going to make it." Sam took her small hands in his, " come" On the far ridge Nadia turns just as Linda's hands reached for her, their eyes met. " I know what you are," she said "and I 'all knock the shit out of you if you try it."

"Sam ? Nadia spoke from the rear of the short column. "How far are we from the main house?"

"Six miles I'd guess."

"You said we would encounter boundaries where are they?"

"Honey," there was an edge to his voice "I don't know, we'll know them when we see them."

" I 'm tired." Janet said, "And I 'm hurting real badly."

Linda looked at her, there was a strange light in her eyes, then unexpected she walked to the child's side and put her arms around her. Jane smiled up at her.

"We're all tired and edgy," Nadia said, "let's take a short break, Sam." But the rest was to be a very short one. Sam had just eased out of the strap of his heavy pack when he heard a sound to his left, slightly behind him. He tensed thumbing the Thompson off safety he spun throwing himself to one side, coming up one knee, the smog leveled on full auto. What he saw numbed him momentarily a demon griffin, a winged horror that until now had been only a part of mythology. The creature charged at Sam, howling as it came. Sam pulled the trigger a one second burst of heavy, 45 caliber slugs. The griffin screamed humanlike and fell to its knees blood gushing out of the holes in its chest and throat. It kicked on the cold forest floor for a few seconds then with a terrible shrieking it beat its wings and died. "What in the name of God is that thing?" Sam asked. Only one amid them knew this answer to that but she had no intention of explaining. it. Nadia screamed, Sam, whirled around, rats had encircled the young girl and Nadia was beating at them with a stick. Linda stood with her back to a tree, her face paled with terror. The rats, much larger and bolder than their earthbound cousins seemly had no fear of humans and no interests in attacking any one other than Janet. The child was kicking at them with her tennis shoes, one of the rodents–leaped at her; yellow teeth snapping. Sam slapped it to the ground and stomped on it with a heavy jump booth smashing the guts from the devilish rodent. He looked up and only then did he see the white slash on the bark of a tree about fifty yards from their rest stop, fifty yards behind them. "Run! Towards that big tree." He pointed, "Get past the tree."

Nadia grabbed Linda and shoved her into action literally forcing her to stop and pick up her pack. The rodents raced back into the forest. Janet looked at the slash on the tree whatever or whoever marked the tree had done so with a mighty sword or a knife wielded with awesome power.

"Those boundaries you people were talking about? I think we found them." Sam lay on the ground sheet, his head resting on his pack. His thoughts were many. It was late afternoon and turning colder, all ready a few flakes of snow had fallen, and it felt as if it might start snowing in earnest at any moment. If that happened he would have to build a fire if we start a fire it might bring some unwelcome visitors, why are they waiting he mused? We are few and they are many and with their powers they must know where we are. Surely they May's be afraid of me?

"Do not flatter yourself so,, young warrior." The voice boomed into Sam's head. "It is I they fear."

"I wondered where you gotten off to." Sam spoke oblivious to the others looking at him, listening to the one sided conversation.

" I have been busy, now hear me young warrior, you must be on guard but you need not fear the evil forces as much as you believe. I will take care of those spawns of hell. They will harass you, worry you, but they won't harm you."

"If you mean, I may kill them, but they May's kill me or us?"

"I didn't say that." Sam sighed an exasperating expulsion of breath.

"Riddles again huh?"

"Only if you believe they are riddles.."

"Is it against the policy of him, for you to come right out and say things in an understandable fashion?"

"How like your father you are, you hedged the question correct. Young warrior" The voice held a slight note of puzzlement "I have spoken to many mortals over these thousands of years but you baffle me."

"How? "

"You aren't afraid of me.

"Why should I be? You're on my side aren't you?"

"And if that force that sits by the right of God, that force of all that is good and pure and just could chuckle it did."

"Confidence is good of course, all great warriors must possess it but don't allow it to cloud your judgment."

" I don't intend to do that. But I will tell you this much, as soon as I get some sign from you, or a feeling is right whatever. I 'm going to Falcon House and kill every one of those coven members." Again Sam got the impression the mighty voice was laughing. Sam held up the Thompson. "I 'all start with this, no telling what I might end up with though."

"Live a good strong healthy productive life offspring of Alex Balloon and when your time on earth is over I will personally welcome you home."

"My time on earth could well be very short."

"That is entirely possible."

"Tell me something, if it is permitted. Am … I recall speaking with you.

Are you Michael? And will I remember any of this if I get out alive. ?"

"You are probing young warrior. . I am forbidden to answer."

"I won't ask why. "

"Wise of one so young."

"Instead I'll ask this when I start my mission? "

"You have wards to look after, lives in your care. A flock if you will, but remember this, sometimes a wolf my disguise itself to enter the flock, and a cabin of evil can sometimes be turned into a fortress of truth. If you so desire you can begin, whenever you are ready." The voice faded Away.

"Sam?" Nadia said watching the young man she loved get to his feet, "what are you going to do?"

"Start a war? The weather was good, and they rested and slept on ground sheets in sleeping bags. Sam had talked long into night with Nadia, with her asking all of what the voice had said.

"There is only one cabin on our land." She told him, "that I know of and I think I would know of any others. It is several miles north of the house. Falcon had it built, its quiet cozy."

Sam glanced at the sun peeking through the timber.

"If we head due west, we should hit the cabin with any luck." he added

" You think that's what the voice was saying?"

"Honey I just don't know I've studied his words over and over. That's the only thing I may think of. As, for that bit a fortress of truth I don't know.

"Well I 'm ready any time you are." She said.

He grinned at her.

"No way," she said, verbally tossing cold water on him..

Chapter Twenty Six

"Ever since we, witnessed that display in the heavens Ralph, you've been moody out of sorts what's the matter honey?"

" You remember I went into town the next morning?"

" Yes"

"Well, I made some phone calls. I made about a dozen phone calls. Charged them on our credit." He grinned ruefully. "Our phone bill for next month should be a real dozy; I called four stargazers in America, one in Canada, the rest overseas and in south America." He looked at his wife when he spoke again his words were soft. "All that activity we watched, the sky changing colors, the palms of dirty-smoke, whatever it was, those odd, unexplainable occurrences, everything Pam. We was the only ones in this world.

"That's impossible!" she protested. "Ralph, it went on for more than an hour! Somebody somewhere has to have seen it."

He solemnly shook his head. "No one I spoke with and I talked with the best people in the business."

"I don't understand, Ralph, we certainly didn't dream what we witnessed, that was a heavenly phenomenon unequalled well by anything I've ever seen or read of. I 'm sorry the cameras malfunctioned and we didn't get it.

"If the camera malfunctioned" he said, "remember the film I shot back at the observatory came out blank as well."

"The people you talked with could be holding back? Deliberately holding back? Maybe to do a paper on the sighting?"

" I thought of that with the first two I spoke with." He confessed, "But a dozen people? No." He sighed.

"So that brings it right back to us." She sat besides him taking his hands in hers "you weren't alone in because sighting several days ago. Why than and not last evening?"

Ralph was silent for a moment; reflecting in his quiet muse. "Don't think me a fool for saying this Pam, and rest assured you will be the only person to ever hear this from my lips, but..."

"All right charge ahead and get it" Said Pam-

"We're Christians, maybe not the best in the world, but we do try. We're believers; let's call it; so perhaps I know I saw the face of God. It was magnificent holy even though he appeared to be quarreling with somebody something, what we witnessed the other night well, have you given any thought to that being from t another world?"

"What other world , Ralph?"

"Hell."

By noon Sam had brought in enough wood to last the women several days, there was plenty of oil for the lamps, candles should they need them, and ample fuel for the portable stoves and lanterns. He took a may have that for his own use there was plenty of canned food in the cabin there was no more Sam could do, but he was hesitant to leave the warmth and safety of the cabin even more hesitant to leave Nadia. Looking at her, sitting quietly in a chair by the fire, Sam realized just how much he loved her, and knew that. That love was right or wrong morally was growing each day she met his tender gaze,.

"It's time for you to go Sam, we'll be all right." she said, "we have weapons and I know how to use them." She blinked away sudden tears, " you have a job to do. Time is growing short I believe."

"Yes," he agreed still reluctant to leave.

"I packed the holy water as carefully as I could. You're sure you have everything else you'll need?" He nodded his head, " I love you Sam."

" And I love you Nadia."

"Go with God," she said her voice breaking.

Without looking back Sam, opened the door and stepped out in the cold air he Quietly closed the door behind him,. He jacked a round into the chamber of the old Thompson slipped the smug on safely and walked down the path heading toward Falcon house the young man had a mission, few would envy. To meet the Devil!

Chapter Twenty Seven

A thousand miles away the coven was resting on the ground in Wheatfield, the members; hundreds of them were exhausted after a night of debauchery torture, and depravity. Their clothing reeked of filth and sin for none-amid them had bathed in weeks, the stink of the devil-worshipers and the smell of rotting flesh hung over the town like an ominous cloud called into being from the drum and canon of a depraved rainmaker. The coven members lay in sleep where they had fallen in exhaustion, stinking breathing heaps of wickedness power of God's retributive wrath toward those who serve another master. Mean while, in Bart house, the four people sat quietly. They listened to a almost too loud ticking of the clock in the hallway, the clay man, was immobile he waited .Jane sat reading the bible, as she was reading she was gaining inner strength for the ordeal that lay ahead of her.

And in firmament the ruler of all things, all plants gave a rumbling command. A dead star sprang into life billions of miles from the planet known as earth. The bit of rock began to glow and smoke and it began its journey slowly. A creature from another time and another world sprang onto the path Sam trod, it roared and clawed at the earth. Sam studied the word of the warrior and he finally understood, he stood his ground glaring at the gluon, a hideous mixture of the hyena and the lion. "You may harm me only if I ceased to believe in God's protection in the house, the few acres around it. And those who live with evil in it are yours, all else is mine, I'm going to destroy the devil's spawn? Yes. Those that are called there are more of those that are called. There are more of those things?" As many as a nonbeliever wishes there to be. He could not tell of the pain that awaited him, could not relate the horror that would confront him, but the warrior felt that the young man would be able to cope. He would be bloodied but with his head not bowed in subservience to that filthy rabble of the Hooded One.

"He's coming." Bill spoke to Falcon using a hand-held walkie-talkie. Falcon knew where Nadia and the others were, just as he knew his master had instructed the bitch to watch out for Nadia's well-being in case Falcon's seed had over powered Sam's weak flow of semen, and she was with Demon as Roma felt her daughter was. Falcon, also knew the fight that Sam was bringing to the grounds was to the death. And the young man was without fear; he was cautioned but, not fearful. Falcon had observed with the help of his master's all powerful eye, the young warrior faced down the gluon, the creature slinking off the timber backs to the hiding place and the old warrior the mighty one's favorite archangel was rubbing his hands together looking forward to a good scrape spoiling for a good fight with God's most hated enemy . The old warrior smiled grimly thinking, I have no need to worry about this young warrior. Then he was off searching the timber. Sword in hand, looking for a fight with the forces of evil. "Johnny!" Falcon roared. "Come here right now." The zombie like living dead shuffled into his earthbound master's quarters. "Young Sam is on the roof sir, got a rifle." Another slug came whining through the house ricocheting off a brick of the fireplace and knocking a jagged hole in the wall. "That son-of-a-bitch!" Falcon cursed him all the while feeling admiration for the young warrior, "by all that is unholy, why couldn't Tom, have turned out like him?"

"Because young Tom is a schemer and a plotter." Johnny replied.

Falcon turned at those words. You know something I need to know Johnny?"

"he plots against you master, with some of the younger members of the coven, I heard them talking, I was listening and they did not see me."

"What did they say Johnny?"

"Young Tom said he had been in communication with the master and he said young Tom could have the coven, should you fail."

"Thank you Johnny. Your snooping finally paid off. I have a task for you. Go to Roma's quarters put her in the center room that is free of windows she must be protected at all time."

" She is with demon child sir?"

"Yes, yes." He said impatiently "then Johnny, as reward for your information tell Judy to come to me I will instruct her that you are to have her at any time you wish."

"Thank you master." Johnny startling drooling, the slobber dripping in stick ropes to the floor.

Sam catnapped from four in the morning until the first red streaks of dawn filtered through the timber. He cautiously moved a mile from his resting place before he squatted down and ate a sandwich. Nadia had fixed him washing it down with cold water from his canteen. With that in his stomach to soften the blow of the pill, Sam took one of Nadia's amphetamines, knowing he had to be alert and knowing he had not had the rest to maintain the vigil he must keep. To stay alive and win this fight he smiled at the carnage that lay on the soft blanket. that was the forest floor the warrior had indeed meant his words when he said he was going to destroy the Devil's spawn. Sam inspected the dead creatures and found them to be as hideous in death as they were in life. So there was some truth to what is mistakenly called mythology, he concluded the scientists and professors and arrogant atheists aren't as wise as they profess to be. "So, what else is new?" He muttered as he left the dead ugliness of the Devil to rot and made his way back to a ridge, this one on the east side of the mansion it was by far the best vantage point he'd found for his shooting distance was shorter and he would be able to see if any one tried to slip from the house, and circle behind him. Smiling he noticed a bell hanging from the rear of the house. Nadia had said it was very a old antique her mother had picked up in Europe,. Sam jacked a round into the heavy, 560, braced himself for the recoiled, and sighted in the bell. 'Ring my bell,' he muttered then gently squeezed the trigger, allowing the weapon to fire itself. The bell clanged, and then jumped from its bracing, blown from the brackets by the force of the heavy slug. But the men and women of the coven trapped inside the mansion were ready for Sam, this time from every window came an Answering volley of shots, forcing Sam to scamper back below the lip of the ridge. He crawled to the slight protection of a small clump of trees and carefully eased his way forward, until he could see the house. He sighted one man firing from the third floor and eased the trigger back. The butt pounded his shoulder but Sam had been shooting downhill, the scope adjusted for that angle and his shot was high not catching the man in the chest, but in the throat, almost decapitating the coven.

The 460 slug flung the man backward his bubbling scream cut off before it could reach his lips. Sliding backward, Sam changed his position, running several hundreds feet before dropping to the earth and easing his way up to the crest of the ridge. He spent the morning harassing those in the mansion but taking no great personal risk in doing so. He knew he would have to go inside the mansion and he was not looking forward to it. For that would put him on Falcon's territory, and the warlock would then have the advantage, but as long as he could , Sam intended to cut the odds down at least make it fifty/ fifty, even-ups the scales tilting in no one's direction.

Jane heard the clock chime its chilling message, the time was noon, odd she thought I've always loved that old clock now, I hate it. Then from the center of the small doomed town, growing stronger and louder with each heartbeat, she listened until she could make out the words that they were chanting. 'Praise him that is our Master' they chanted, 'now the Christian whore dies praise the Hooded One' the chant was repeated over and over, until it became a maddened drone in Jane's head. She looked for the mist that was Alex and was not surprised to find him gone, he had warned her, and she would have to face some of the ordeal alone. She stood, moving to the front door, she had taken a long hot bath, fixed her hair and done her nails she had put on her best dress, and her jewelry and now she stood facing the door, her bible in her hand, waiting...

"Why does this have to be?" Bart asked the misty face of Balloon. The Mist stirred but projected no reply. "I will if not gladly certainly willingly take her place." Wayne said.

"And I know I speak for all here. We've all talked about it that cannot be why, for God's sake? "Anita asked.

"Precisely, the reason."

"Alex you're speaking in riddles," Bart accused him.

"No you do perceive them as puzzles that are all."

"She's dying for us, isn't she Alex?" Betty asked.

"Yes. "

"But there is more to it than that, isn't there Alex?"

"She's dying for you isn't she Alex?" Bart's words were softly spoken and not accusatory when Balloon thrust in the reply the one word was charged with emotion.

"Yes!"

The long filthy line of Satanists stopped in front of the house. The chanting ceased the town grew quiet, "hey, Bitch!"A man's husky voice called out. "Get your ass out of that house. It's your time."

"Yeah." Another called "and you might as well step out of them panties fore you do, cause you going to be out of them damn quick." Ugly laughter rang in Jane's ears. The small petite lady stepped out of her house onto the porch, seized by dirty rough, hands, manhandle profanely. As if envious of her neat appearance a woman reached out and quickly mussed her hair, hard hands roamed over her body. "Take her to the circle of stones." Jean command the digging, she stood in front of Jane with hate shinning in her dark eyes , she spat in Jane's face, the spittle dripping from the smaller woman's cheek. "It's going to be fun listening to you beg Christian cunt.

Jane's reply was calm. "That will never happen I May's say I won't scream but I may assure you, with the love of God in my heart I will never beg."

Jean slapped her backward. Take her. Laying on the ridge, facing the house Something very cold touched Sam's heart. His big hands gripped the rifle until his fingers ached from the strain." Muter," he whispered. The scene in Wheatfield was suddenly played before his eyes a five-second burst of reality. Then it vanished as quickly as it appeared. Sam put his forehead on the ground and allowed himself the denied luxury of tears. A rifle shot from the house spitting dirt onto his face brought him back to his own reality; the young man cut his eyes upward. " I guess you have your reasons," she wondered how long she had been here .Wondered if it was hours or days another man fell on her bruised nakedness spreading her legs forcing his way into her grunting his dubious pleasure as he worked in and out of her. Jane had learned early on that to fight them only meant more pain, with the result being the same better not resist she opened her eyes, watching the last of the sun's rays fade on color beyond the western horizon, she had stopped counting the men assaulting her when she reached twenty and there had been many more after that.

Chapter Twenty Eight

"You have twenty-four hours, young warrior." The heavy voice boomed into Sam's brain, "forget the tablet, for it is gone."

"Where is it?"

"Taken by the Dark One."

"Then he must know, he is going to lose here?"

"He never loses entirely. Something of importance to him will have been gained here delivered elsewhere bursting forth on this earth. Perhaps twice but time is growing short"

"Twenty-four-hours young warrior, that is all you have, but one other thing you must be gone from this place, by the twenty-second hour do not ask me why that must be. You have a task before you. Good-luck young warrior." Sam leaned back against a tree trunk, his mind racing, tossing out ideas and plans almost as soon as they formed only one course of action was certain, he had to go inside the mansion. Sam needed sleep, but was afraid to doze for fear they would find him and kill him. His eyes closed resting for a moment. Exhaustion quickly overcame anxiety and the young man slept. The mightiest of all warriors was bemused as he watched over his young charge. 'Sleep for a few hours, young warrior' he thought, 'I will bend the rules a bit and watch over you. Bending the rules is not that uncommon for me.'

Jane, lay on her back on the dark alter, blood from her torn anus staining the dark evil stone. She shifted position softly whimpering as pain cut through her, 'beg for mercy from your God!' Jean and the others had screamed at her while Jay anally assaulted her. But Jane had shaken her head 'no,' all the while biting her lips against the pain, being forced in and out of her when Jay was finished, another took his place then another, it seemed never to stop. Jane wept when, Tony stepped forward, 'I've always wanted it this way, with you Jane.' Tony said, "But you never would let me, do you remember?" His words had been barley audible over the waves of pain washing over her. He mounted her laughing at her cries of pain. 'Good, isn't it!' he shouted at her. The rape had finally stopped for a time then someone brought a artificial penis to Jean, they wanted to degrade Jane in everyway that they could the coven leader strapped it on. It's better to give than to receive she said. And now the words Jane feared were spoken, 'let the black mass begin' Jean said, 'well body receive this.' Jane passed out from the pain.

Jean said, "Bring the virgin child to the circle." Jane was jerked from the stone alter and shoved naked into the hands of the coven members still their fingers would not stop seeking the opening of her body, finally they tied her hands behind her back, the rope cutting into her flesh. They forced her to kneel before the alter as the black mass began. The coven members sang their praises to the Dark One. Jane with a smile on her lips sang God's hymns in a soft sweet voice, which seemed to carry above the chanting of the hundreds of voices. Her singing infuriated Jean, A woman running to the naked, kneeling Christian, slapping her across her mouth, back handing her, attempting to still the voice singing praises to a God Jean had rejected years before. But even with blood from smashed lips leaking down her chin dripping onto bear bruised breasts could not silence her.. Jean became wild with fury striking at Jane with bullied fists. Jane slumped to the ground bright lights popping like painful flashes in her brain. "Shut your goddamned filthy fucking mouth Christian whore!" Jean screamed, "Will one of you men come here and stick a cock in her mouth!" One did ramming his maleness into Jane mouth. Jane bit him clamping down like a bulldog hanging on with all the tenacity of a Mississippi river snapping turtle. The man screamed and howled in pain as Jane spat out part of the man's pride and joy. Jean kicked her in the stomach. Jane fought for breath gagging and retching on the ground. A small girl was led crying and whimpering to the black alter Jane recognized the child as the daughter of a friend. Alice was eleven years old. Jane struggle to her knees speaking around the blood in her mouth, she told the child'

" All I may do is pray for you. I may do nothing else for you Alice." The man now who only possessed only half a penis was still screaming in pain as she was led away. "Oh, no Alice." Jean said patting the girl's head she may save you all the pain and hurt, yes, she may just ask her."

The child turned anguished eyes to the bound naked woman kneeling in the dirt.

"Do it Jane. Please."

"You rotten Bitch!" Jane cursed Jean.

The woman laughed and spat at her. "Ball's in your court now, miss prissy all you have to do is renounce your faith in your God and the kid goes free and the message comes straight from the Dark One's lips."

" I will not deny my God." Jane said, "And he will not deny me,"

"Listen to the little cunt screamed for a few hours, bitch you might change your mind."

"No." Jane said quietly "I will not."

And the crowd surged forward all straining to see the girl raped and tortured and offered up to their Dark Master in sacrifice. Jane had thought the pitiful weeping and screaming of the child would never cease and she knew she had never prayed so hard in her life until now. Just before the hideous sacrifice was to begin a chosen mender would literally slice strips of flesh from the girl. The child shuddered, gasped once and died the blank empty eyes staring at nothing.

Jean looked to the heavens and said "thank you."

"You had something to do with her death, break all her fingers now. One at a time makes her beg." Jane laid on the ground her useless hands by her side. She had wept but she did not beg. She had been dragged to the darkness of the inner circle forced to watch as the beasts ate the body of the young child.

There was grudging respect in Jean's eyes as she probed Jane awake with the toe of her boot. It had suddenly turned cold in Fork County the temperature had started to dropping Satan had pulled away his presence. Jane, Lay shivering naked on the ground, but she had neither complained nor begged.

"You think you've won don't you?" Jean asked her, lips pulled in a sneer

"Yes," Jane managed a whisper pushing the word past swollen lips "my God always does."

Jean squatted down besides her, the stench of her unwashed body unbearable, she pulled a hunting knife from a sheath, "what I think I'll do bitch, is cut off your tits and feed them to the beasts." Jane said nothing, "you wouldn't beg even then would you"?

"No" the suffering ravaged her.

"You know what we're going to do don't you? yes." Jean stood. Looked at Jane for a moment, and then savagely kicked her in the face with a booted foot. "Get the cross." She said to Jay, "and the hammers and spikes do it now."

"Is it almost over, Alex? Bart asked

"Please God let it be."

"A few more hours. Then you'll stop suffering It will be stopped.

"I still don't understand why it had to be." Betty said.

"Not entirely it will be explained I promise."

"You left us several times last night," Bart said "I felt your presence leave.."

"I went to the scene of ugliness several times. Once I let the spirit of the child departs her body."

Betty asked, "You could do that for her, and not for Jane."

"Yes."

"There is so much I do not understand."

"It will be explained."

Behind Wayne the curtain of life or death assigned, "I never thought I'd hear myself say this but I 'm ready to go." Bart pointed to Wayne "not me,."

"Soon" the mist that was Balloon told them, "only a few more hours."

"Oh," Bart moaned.

She had screamed when they drove the spikes into her hands and feet. Then awake she found the strength to cope, they had jammed a crown of thorns on her head, the blood dripped down her face streaking her bruised beauty. She hung naked from her wooden tower, "tell me your God is shit!" Tony yelled up at her. Her eyes found him. "My God is love "Jane whispered.

"Tell us you renounce your Faith in your God and we'll get you down, tend your wounds."

Jane managed a smile shaking her head, "no."

Some of the crowd grew restless, worried as this was not going as planned. They had beaten and rape and tortured her , nailed her to the cross and she still kept her faith some began questioning their minds could they under the same circulation retain their faith for the Hoofed One? Many doubted it. "I want out a woman sobbed. Oh, God help me get away from here." A few others joined her 'take Jane down!' A man called out 'she's suffered enough.' Those few were seized and killed one was spread-eagled on the ground a stake driven through his stomach he lay screaming for hours another man was given to the beasts, the beasts ate him alive. Two of the women were raped then given to the beasts for breeding purposes the woman who first cried out was given to Jay, she screamed out her humiliation as he took her in various ways. Then she was stoned to death.

"Any One else want out?" Jean demanded shouting at the crowd. "If so, just step forward." Jane watched them sensing the mood of many shifting she wanted to tell them that if they admitted their sins and accepted God as the only true God they could be saved.

"Don't concern yourself with them!" Balloon's word cut through the pain in her body, they are filth, rabble, body and soul belonging to the Dark One.

"They are sinners of the most evil sort knowingly willingly lovingly violating all God's Commandments. After all the pain and torture that they put you through you want to save them."

"Yes! And the Firmament." Balloon said, "very well."

It was five O'clock Saturday; Sam darted across the grounds toward the growing darkness. No lights showing, dark windows like evil watching eyes. Stopping at the back door he paused to catch his breath and to ponder his sanity at doing this. Putting an ear to the door he listened but could detect no sound from within, he drew back extending his arm to the door knob, just before his hand touched the brass, the door swung open glistering wetly in the darkness of the room. "My dear .Mr. Balloon." the warlock said with a smile "we've been waiting."

." Stay away from me," Janet warned the older girl, "I mean it."

"I don't trust you." she whispered "why don't you scream? Nadia will come to your aid."

"I will if you don't leave me alone."

Nadia lay on the couch before the fire, deep in sleep her stomach was hurting she moaned in her sleep. Linda was steadily backing the child into a corner her face holding a strange look, eyes burning "really thought you could get away with it didn't you?"

"I don't know what you are talking about." Janet's hand closed around the poker in the corner, "I 'm your friend and you know what I mean, open your shirt." Linda command, "I want to see the mark you have on you."

"You're crazy," the child hissed her fear.

"I want to see if you are marked, if you are really one of us. Come too me now!" A dull splattering sound filled the room. Nadia awakened to screaming.

"It's good" Jean spoke to the coven." We' have been assured a long exciting Life here on earth this act guarantees it.

Behind them , all around the circle of stones, around and slightly beneath the height of Jane's lonely perch, a low moaning sobbing sound was heard, the anguished sounds of pain and prayer, audibly mixing with silent flicker of torches that lit the scene of awfulness some of the men, and women who had repented to the true way had been crucified, some had been stripped naked and the skin peeled from their living bodies, others had been sexually mutilated and left to bleed to death. All the women and some of the men had been sexually hideously. But not one had renounced the Lord God. "Good-bye Sam," Jane spoke to her son.

"Always remember that your mother loves you."

The words slammed into Sam's brain as he stood in the doorway. "Good-bye Mother," he said flinging his thoughts with all the strength he could muster. Sam's head was once again clear, he felt new strength enter he looked at Falcon, "you may save yourself a great deal of pain young man." The warlock said "with just one simple act,"

"And that is?"

"Renounce your God."

"I have something to say to that." Sam returned the mocking smile.

" Yes young man?" And just before Sam hit the warlock smack in the mouth, dropping him to the floor momentarily stunning the man he said "fuck you!" Sam was past the dining area and into the den running hard before Falcon could pull himself up from the floor, vile smelling blood leaking from his bruised mouth. The young man charged the room full of Satanist startling them, holding the Thompson smug firm, swinging it left to the right. Sam blew a half dozen of them into the arms of their master, and then charged through the house running up the first flight of steps leading to Roma's room. He had several sharpened stakes shoved behind his belt, turning at the landing by the second flight of stairs Sam ended the life of seven more, emptying the drum into them as they charged recklessly behind him a bloody path. His arms burned from the lead but it was not serious. He ran up the stairs. Lana confronted him, hissing at him, teeth fanged, fingers turned into talons reaching for him her breath stinking. He fired into her body and she flopped on the floor screaming oaths at him, but she would not die yet, she crawled to her feet mouth and tongue blood-red just as Sam tore off a vial of holy water and flung it at her. The water bubbled and hissed, as it burned her face and body searing and smoking as the acid eating into her dead but unholy flesh. She screamed and thrashed on the floor beating her feet to a macabre dark pain and death. Furious footsteps sounded behind him. Sam spun around, ejected the drum and rammed home another clip jacking a round into the chamber. He crouched at the ready, as several youthful members of he coven all from the Barrington college came rushing at him.

Sam pulled the trigger back and held it, starting the hard burst waist high. One slug caught him on the hipbone, flinging him backward over the railing he screamed as he flew through the air, the screaming abruptly halted when he hit the marble floor he spattered with an ugly sound. The hallway was littered with dead and dying and undead bodies. Sam doused them with blessed water and raced to Roma's room the screaming smoking flesh fowling the air behind him. Roma was gone, her room empty. Sam ran through the three suites pausing to look at a picture on a dresser by a rumble bed. It was a 8x10 photo of his father. Sam stood for what seen like five minutes but, he had a feeling that time was spinning past him and he did not understand that. The picture seemed to hold him mesmerized he was conscious of a strange stillness in the great house. Nothing was moving at all then he shook his disbelieving eyes the photograph melted into something. He spun at a noise behind him. Tom stood a dueling sword in each hand. "I will guarantee my position of greatest, by your death at My hands he said smiling. We will fight fairly you and I with these he held the slim sword you mortals have a streak of justness inherently in you, so I know we bled and we shall have a fair fight shall we begin brother?"

"If you'd ever gone through Ranger school you would know that you just ask a very stupid question, shall we begin to the death brother! "

Sam shifted the Thompson and blew a dozen holes into Tom. Tom was flung backward slamming against the wall, the bullet holes in his chest, but he would not die he slowly rose to his feet laughing insanely, "you don't fight fair brother." He said, flicking the tip of the sword at Sam.

"Isn't that the truth? Sam said

Tom shrieked and started thrashing on the floor he was unable to get up this time, he heard footsteps on the stairs, doors slamming boots on the steps running, He jerked a stake out of his belt and drove it into Tom's chest. The odor of stinking pus engulfed him, as Tom lay dying on the floor. "One point I must make dear brother," he gashed as life ebbed from him. Have you taken into consideration that one day your wife might turn on you, will you shoot her too for we are the same." Tom managed to say.

"Fire, someone yelled! The house on fire." Sam ran to the balcony and opened fire on the coven members knocking several of them spinning and howling to the floor. He ran down the hallways setting rooms blazing quitting only when he ran out, fire.

Chapter Twenty-Nine

"And matches it May's be this easily."

"You are quiet right young man,"

He held his Thompson ready to fire his

"Oh, for pity sake" Falcon said, "put that thing away for it cannot harm me unlike your brother, I've been shot by many a jealous husbands."

Sam looked at his watch.

"Why do you keep looking at your watch? Are you expecting company?" Falcon asked.

"What?"

"Your watch and the expression on your face, ah." comprehension flooded his featured, " I see the ancient warrior gave you a timetable did he not ? Where are all the others, you have been going around charging at everything. You May's win fighting me."

Sam, held on to the two vials of holy water he threw one vile of holy water on Falcon, The warlock started to screamed, "you lose young man," Falcon said

"You lose, you mean Falcon,"

H he had began to gurgle from the smoking hole in his throat. Falcon could no longer talk, his throat a burning a hole, emitting putrid odors of the grave and beyond, he slowly pulled a flat automatic pistol from his jacket pocket and pulled the trigger twice, both slugs hitting Sam, in the chest and stomach. Sam tumbled forward down the steps. He rolled next to Falcon; , his blood mixing with the slime oozing from the Warlock's rotting burning flesh. s Strength was leaving him. He collapsed as darkness enveloped him, falling into the oozing slime.

"Get into the car," Balloon projected, "everybody! Now!"

" I will bring the clay man, wait just one moment?" Bart said.

" That golem weighs half a ton, if you ask me. I almost gave myself a hernia fooling with it."

"Just don't you start arguing wit me?" Bart sighed

"And what do we do when we get in the car?"

" We are supposed to go to do the digging, for that is where it all began ,we will be waiting for you there , so I guess this is it than ?"

"Yes. Oh, Bart said, putting one hand to his mouth." All ready I 'm starting to feel strange."

"Bart," his wife said, "be quiet all right,."

"Alex I 'm ready, let's go."

"Betty" her husband said, "don't be in such a hurry when you get to the digging. Walk toward the crosses you won't be seen or bothered."

Epilogue

Sam felt hands on him, and he tried to fight off, finally giving up, he was too weak. He opened his eyes and looked into the face of Nadia, he was so very glad to see her beautiful face and in her eyes was pure love, "you'll have to help us honey."

"What do you mean us?

"Janet is here with me."

"Where's Linda? "

"Dead she was one of them too; I told you long ago that there was something wrong with her..'

When Wayne and the others drove up to the old dig site what they witnessed was the end of the coven. The golem was indestructible and awesome in his fury. Not even when dozen of Devil-worshipers, charged the clay man could they move him, stop him, or even slow him down in his killings frenzy.

"We're supposed to walk through all that and not be noticed .I just don't get it."

" I do, said Wayne "because we're not here any more old friend.

"Are you trying to tell me that we're all ready dead?"

" Yes."

"Yes" Balloon said.

"Behind them you are free of this earth, walk toward the crosses" they walked across the digging site, littered with the broken bodies of those who choose to live with the Dark One. Bart, stopped for one moment as he spun around and saw an old friend, " hey, you owe me for that living room set you brought from me ten years ago." The man went screaming down the street the four walked through the scene of blood and pain , past the golem who was occupied solely in tearing them apart. They walked to a petite figure standing besides the tallest cross, under the ravaged pale naked body of Jane besides the figure dressed in a white robe, her hair shining in the glow of the Torches, her complexion unmarred by bruises, beautiful and radiant.

"Come on." Alex said "it is finally over, come on we must go. Time is short and growing shorter by the minute." Far down a strange–appearing road that angled softly, gently upward they could see a line of people walking they were finally happy and laughing at long last. Wayne took his wife's hand together hand in hand they walked up the road with Alex and Jane..

"Don't look back, keep your eyes straight ahead." f

"Yes."Alex Balloon said, his hand seeking and finding Jane and the two were together forever at long last.

When the golem's work was done he began his lumbering walk to the river miles from the scene of defilement, at the river the clay man stepped down the bank and stood there. He slowly melted into the earth and became once more that which he was all things of this earth a creation of God, with the almighty once more reclaiming him. The fireball seared the land leaving nothing but smoke and ruin and fire, the land would one day grow again bits of grass popping up flowers blooming seeking the warmth of the sun. It would it be a long time, and when the first flower would appear pushing out of the earth toward God's sun it would be blood red.

The doctor's in a small English hospital came out of the operation room a smile on his lips. "He's going to be all right," he told the young woman standing besides the bed..

"Thank God" Nadia said tears, rolling down her face.

In a small Mexico settle in Western Europe a woman died giving birth. No doctor was in attendance. The baby did not birth normally it literally exploded from the womb in a gush of blood and mangled flesh. Roma screamed for the last time as the gaping wound in her stomach tore the life from her. She saw only a glimpse of the infant before she finally died but that one quick look was enough . She died with a smile on her lips, knowing she had served her master well.

They allowed an old woman to hold it for a time, the old woman's who just birthed a child was brought in to nurse, the infant, the nursing mother like her mother and all others in attendance wore a strange looking medallion around her neck . The child, after nursing played with the medallion. In the caves, behind the charred remains, of the once great mansion called the Devil's House the beasts settled in for a long sleep, they had kept a very low profile during the battles among good and evil forces and the old warrior. They knew when to fight and when not to fight. Now they slept with only a singly sentry on guard. They would be called again they always were.

And on the sixth day of the sixth month Nadia gave birth to a beautiful baby boy. Janet was returned to her parents. The marks on Nadia's neck had long healed.

Janet walked over to the window, away from everyone else and stared

Out, she stood for a few moments looking at her reflection in the mirror and started to smile. She smiled the parting of young lips exposing teeth suddenly fanged the points glistering sharply blood-red. Her eyes were wild, that of a person who was possessed the wild look vanishes from her face, the teeth were again normal.

The young girl turned around facing the adults. "I don't know what I would have done without Sam and Nadia? I owe both of you my life. I promised you I 'all look after the baby. Forever and ever."

She smiled very sweetly!

www.ingramcontent.com/pod-product-compliance
Lightning Source LLC
LaVergne TN
LVHW090610110826
845146LV00001B/334

* 9 7 8 1 4 2 6 9 3 4 4 0 7 *